Never Before Had Lainie Taken So Much As A Moment To Think About Getting Married And Having A Child.

Rocking a baby, watching it grow were things she'd refused to consider.

She'd been so wrapped up in her career, so busy getting ahead that she hadn't given a family of her own a second thought.

Lainie blinked back wetness. She slid a glance over at Sloan's profile, wondering what he thought about having kids.

She chastised herself for being an idiot. Know a guy for three days, share one spectacular dance and an equally spectacular kiss and you start thinking of diapers and baby blankets? That was just the sort of thing she counseled against in her column. She'd told literally hundreds of women not to do anything so foolish.

Good thing she and Sloan had only shared kisses.

Oh, but she wanted to share so much more....

Dear Reader,

Welcome back to another passionate month at Silhouette Desire. A *Scandal Between the Sheets* is breaking out as Brenda Jackson pens the next tale in the scintillating DYNASTIES: THE DANFORTHS series. We all love the melodrama and mayhem that surrounds this Southern family—how about you?

The superb Beverly Barton stops by Silhouette Desire with an extra wonderful title in her bestselling series THE PROTECTORS. *Keeping Baby Secret* will keep *you* on the edge of your seat—and curl your toes all at the same time. What would you do if you had to change your name and your entire history? Sheri WhiteFeather tackles that compelling question when her heroine is forced to enter the witness protection program in *A Kept Woman*. Seems she was a kept woman of another sort, as well…so be sure to pick up this fabulous read if you want the juicy details.

Kristi Gold has written the final, fabulous installment of THE TEXAS CATTLEMAN'S CLUB: THE STOLEN BABY series with *Fit for a Sheikh*. (But don't worry, we promise those sexy cattlemen with be back.) And rounding out the month are two wonderful stories filled with an extra dose of passion: Linda Conrad's dramatic *Slow Dancing With A Texan* and Emilie Rose's supercharged *A Passionate Proposal*.

Enjoy all we have to offer this month—and every month—at Silhouette Desire.

Melissa Jeglinski

Melissa Jeglinski
Senior Editor, Silhouette Desire

Please address questions and book requests to:
Silhouette Reader Service
U.S.: 3010 Walden Ave., P.O. Box 1325, Buffalo, NY 14269
Canadian: P.O. Box 609, Fort Erie, Ont. L2A 5X3

Slow Dancing With a Texan

LINDA CONRAD

Silhouette® Desire

Published by Silhouette Books

America's Publisher of Contemporary Romance

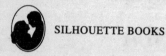

SILHOUETTE BOOKS

ISBN 0-373-76577-0

SLOW DANCING WITH A TEXAN

This edition published by arrangement with Harlequin Books S.A.

® and TM are trademarks of Harlequin Books S.A., used under license. Trademarks indicated with ® are registered in the United States Patent and Trademark Office, the Canadian Trade Marks Office and in other countries.

Visit Silhouette at www.eHarlequin.com

Printed in U.S.A.

LINDA CONRAD

Born in Brazil to a commercial pilot and his wife, Linda Conrad was raised in south Florida and has been a dreamer and storyteller for as long as she can remember. After her mother's death a few years ago, she moved from her then-home in Texas to Southern California and gave up her previous life as a stockbroker to rededicate herself to her first love—writing.

Linda and her husband, along with a Siamese mix cat named Sam, recently moved back to south Florida. She's been writing contemporary romances for about five years and loves sharing them with readers. She enjoys growing roses, reading cozy mysteries and sexy romances, and driving her little convertible in the sunshine. But most important, Linda loves learning about—and living with—passion.

It makes Linda's day to hear from readers. Visit with her at www.LindaConrad.com.

One

Danged, crazy-fool redhead.

With one swift curse under his breath, Texas Ranger Sloan Abbott checked his watch and headed across the narrow downtown street toward the lobby where the foolhardy woman stood in full view. He wasn't supposed to meet Lainie Gardner in her office on the twelfth floor of the *Houston News* building for another half hour.

He'd had serious reservations about taking this assignment. Being a bodyguard wasn't his normal area of expertise. But he knew enough to be sure that a stalking victim was supposed to follow instructions.

Her life might depend on it.

Sloan had spent the day inspecting every inch of the building and the surrounding area. He knew the elevator systems and the location of each closet and air duct. No one could've done a better job of securing the premises than he had.

He'd also spent a good deal of time studying a dossier on Ms. Gardner that the captain had given him. The surprise was that he'd been fascinated by the interesting bits and pieces the file had supplied of her life.

Sloan had already come to the conclusion it would definitely be worthwhile to postpone the trip that had been the original reason he'd taken a leave of absence from the Texas Rangers. Protecting a beautiful advice columnist seemed like a much better idea at the moment than searching out potentially painful truths about his background.

So what does the gorgeous woman with such a famous face do? She casually strolls out of the elevator into the open lobby in full daylight.

He'd had no trouble recognizing her from across the street. Of course, he'd been studying her pictures. But he also knew that for years her face had been splattered in newspapers as an advertisement for her syndicated advice columns. With her flash of bright-copper hair, she'd be hard for anyone to miss.

As irritated as he was with her casual behavior, he couldn't help the smile that broke out on his face when he walked closer to the reality of Lainie Gardner—despite how foolish she was being at the moment.

The pictures hadn't done her justice. Her body was compact, sturdy but curved in all the right places. And even dressed as she was, in loose-fitting pants and a sweater, he could tell that most of her five-foot, seven-inch body was made up of long, sexy legs.

Have mercy. He'd always been a leg man.

His mood changed dramatically when he saw Lainie stop in full view of the street and begin to laugh at something the other woman said. She'd been told to wait in her office until he arrived to give her instructions and escort her home. She was in danger and had been threatened. So what the hell was she doing?

He heard the muffled crack at the same instant the glass in front of him fractured into a million crystal slivers and flew in every direction. Someone screamed. Someone else shouted. But Sloan didn't waste time wondering where the shot had come from.

After sprinting through the shattered window, he pushed past hysterical bystanders to the spot where the two women lay. Both of them were facedown on the marble floor…and there was blood. Lots of blood.

Within two seconds he'd determined that both women were still alive and that Lainie hadn't lost consciousness. She didn't fight him, as he pulled her up and quickly decided to remove her from the line of fire. If she was hurt badly, he'd find out soon enough. But for now, he wasn't taking any chances on her being shot again while he stopped to check her wounds.

Another sudden hail of bullets had bystanders dodging out of the way to the sidewalk. "Call 9-1-1!" he shouted to anyone within earshot.

But Sloan was sure that, when he got Lainie out

of sight, the shooting would stop. She had to be the target.

It was a danged good thing he'd checked this building out earlier. Sloan dashed into an alcove and found the side exit to an employee parking lot.

He stopped at the door and gently lowered her to the floor. Kneeling beside her, he checked her pulse and looked for any obvious or bleeding wounds. Her eyes fluttered open and he saw the shock in her eyes, but he didn't see pain.

Relieved, Sloan carefully opened the heavy metal door and scrutinized the lot. It seemed quiet enough, but he knew that in the brilliant sunlight of the late afternoon their chances of making it to his pickup without being seen were pretty slim. He lifted her again and laid her across his shoulder in preparation to make a run for it.

She moaned and squirmed. "My…my sister. Please help her."

"Stay still! Don't move," he ground out in a whisper. "Someone will be coming to help the others. You're still in danger."

A second later he slid them both past the protection of the door and dashed toward the alley where he'd parked. He managed to make it across the asphalt lot without incident by darting between the parked cars.

"Wait a minute!" she yelled as she grabbed the back of his shirt with both hands. "Stop. I can't…"

He ignored her words because he didn't want to waste his running breath, but he was grateful that her voice sounded so strong. Maybe she hadn't been hit at all. He needed a peaceful moment to stop and really check her over.

Until then he had mere seconds to decide whether stealth or speed was their best chance at survival. Quickly making the decision to get the hell out of Dodge as fast as possible, Sloan punched the button on his keyless entry remote and heard the familiar but noisy beeps coming from his pickup in the alleyway twenty feet beyond.

He'd never before realized how loud and echoing the sound of the alarm-disengage truly was. Too late now.

Sloan all but threw her into the front seat and slammed the door. He made it clear around to the driver's side and had the key in the ignition before hearing the ping of bullets as they hit the asphalt behind them.

"Stay down," he snapped at her.

"I have to go back." She popped her head up as he gunned the engine. "My sister...all the others... they need help. I have to help them."

"The police will take care of it. But you've got to keep low." He pushed at her shoulder while the truck screamed out of the alley.

Lainie banged her head on the glove box as she slid off the seat like a rag doll and landed on the dirty floor mat below. She let loose a string of very unladylike remarks and struggled to hang on.

The engine revved and the tires squealed as the truck jerked madly around a corner. What in heaven's name was happening to her?

Taking a deep breath, she opened her eyes and chanced a glimpse at the crazy cowpoke who'd manhandled her into this predicament. At once Lainie took in the shiny, leather cowboy boots and the spotless white Western hat.

Almost chalking him up to being an out-of-control urban cowboy, she briefly wondered if this was a kidnapping. Before that thought registered, he dragged at the wheel and sent the pickup truck into a spin.

It couldn't have been more than two seconds later when he grimaced and righted the wheel again. But in that instant, she'd managed a glimpse under his denim jacket of a freshly starched white Western-cut shirt, a dark blue tie and the silver badge pinned neatly over his breast pocket.

Just then she remembered. Her mother had said to expect Captain Chet Johnson's handpicked man this afternoon. What was the man's name? Oh, yes. Sergeant Sloan Abbott of the Texas Rangers.

"We've got a black van on our tail." His eyes flicked to the rearview mirror.

"Someone is following us?" she rasped. "But why?"

He shot her a quick, dark look that could've easily pinned her to the dashboard. "If it's somehow managed to escape your notice, people have been shooting at you for the last ten minutes."

Lainie thought about the cracking sound she'd heard when the whole world exploded around her. She'd been standing in the lobby, chuckling over some joke her sister had told when they'd heard the noise. Both she and Suzy had hit the floor in the same instant. So it must've been gunfire that broke the glass window next to them.

Suzy. My goodness, what had happened to her?

"Please," she yelled over the roar of the engine and the screech of tires. "The others...we have to make sure they're okay. Turn around."

"The HPD are there by now," he muttered without looking in her direction. "And probably the paramedics. I heard the sirens. They can handle them a lot better than we can." He dragged at the wheel again and the truck slid around a corner.

Whoa! Her questions would have to wait, as the ride got rougher and she had to fight to maintain her balance. Lainie moved her arm to get a better hold on the seat as the truck rocketed into a left turn. She gasped when she caught a glimpse of her own bloodstained sleeve.

The lawman's head jerked around at the sound. "Where are you injured?" He'd obviously spotted the blood, too.

"I...I don't know. I...don't think I am." She wasn't sure. Trying to concentrate on both her body and her balance, she'd discovered that her arms and legs were definitely cramped by being shoved under the dashboard. But the rest of her mostly just felt numb.

"The van's side windows are blacked out but I think I can see at least three of them through the front," he yelled, not waiting for the rest of her answer. "I'm going to lose them. Another block and we'll hit the freeway on-ramp. Can you stay put until then, Lainie?"

She didn't think she had much choice, so she nodded her head. He'd called her Lainie. It gave her a solid, calming feeling to hear him say her name. She realized that anyone might know who she was from reading her daily column. But still, this man's very presence said he was a lawman—her very own Texas Ranger bodyguard.

"You're Sloan Abbott, aren't you?"

He nodded his answer but didn't take the time to speak. The truck tires squealed in protest as he made one more fast right turn. She was sincerely relieved she hadn't been able to see that maneuver.

The truck accelerated as she felt it travel up a hill. They'd apparently hit a freeway on-ramp, but she couldn't be sure which one. The newspaper's office was located within a few minutes of a half-dozen different interstates near downtown Houston. But since she couldn't see out the windows, she had no idea of where they were.

Sloan suddenly reached his long arm over and grabbed her by the front of her sweater, pulling her up and onto the seat. "Buckle up, Ms. Gardner."

Lainie yelped in protest at being so roughly buffeted, but she turned around and did exactly what she'd been told. After buckling her seat belt, she hung on to the door handle with one hand while bracing herself against the seat with the other. The scenery whizzed by in a blur.

She wasn't sure she could catch her breath, and silently begged him to stop this madness and pull over. When he did, she owed him a piece of her mind. His driving was scarier than whoever was chasing them.

He whirled his truck past a few speeding cars as if they were standing still, whipping in and out of all three lanes. Lainie checked him out with a speculative glance.

His jaw was set, his dark eyes concentrated on the road. But even in profile, she could see he was easy to look at. If it had been any other time, she'd be interested in getting to know a man who looked as good as this one. With a hard but handsome face, he looked strong and slightly dangerous. Just the way a lawman should. The thought gave her a little thrill, but this wasn't the time for that, either.

She watched him check the rearview mirror again, and automatically shot a glance behind her through the back window. Sure enough, a plain black van was keeping up with them, just a few cars back.

Yikes! Was this whole thing really connected to the nasty letters she'd been receiving? Lainie had thought they were just a joke—one in very bad taste to be sure, but not terribly scary.

The Houston Police Department hadn't thought this stalker business was very serious, either. Because, although they'd taken statements from Lainie, her staff and family, the police told her there wasn't too much they could do unless the writer made an overt move to harm someone. That practical stance had seemed reasonable at the time.

But all this shooting and chasing was certainly overt enough for her now. Silently she thanked heaven for her mother's old friend, Chet Johnson. At least he'd taken the threat seriously enough to insist on finding a man to be her bodyguard in his off-duty hours.

The idea of a bodyguard had initially seemed silly. She didn't have time or the patience for such nonsense. In fact, she'd been surprised that her mother made such a big deal over something she'd considered so unimportant.

Maybe Lainie would consider apologizing to her mom now. But it still seemed a little overboard.

"Pros," he hissed through gritted teeth. "Hang on. We're about to shake them loose."

He put his foot on the gas and sped out of the left

lane, making the next exit ramp on two wheels and with no room to spare. Without bothering to stop for the light at the bottom of the ramp, he made two quick left turns and headed up the on-ramp going in the opposite direction.

Positive they must've lost the van with that move, Lainie caught her breath. Looking into the setting sun, she realized for the first time that they'd been heading east toward Louisiana. And now they were headed…where? Back to the city?

"Where are we going?" she croaked past a dry mouth.

Ignoring her question, he reached inside his jacket and pulled out a mobile phone. He punched in one number, then threw her a narrowed look as he spoke.

She overheard him making some reference to her and the Houston police, and guessed that he was speaking to his boss, Captain Johnson. Lainie was desperate to speak to Chet, too.

"Right. Code twenty-seven. Got it," he said into the phone. Then he flipped it shut and stashed it.

"Wait! I wanted to talk to him." She swiveled in her seat and glared at the side of Sloan's head.

"Sorry." He didn't turn but continued to pay attention to the road ahead. "The captain said the Houston police want to talk to us, but they're going to have to wait until tomorrow. It's too risky for you to show up at one of the substations right now. Too obvious."

"But you didn't ask about my sister. I have to know what happened to her…to everyone." Lainie was unaccustomed to being out of control.

"The most important thing now is to get you out of sight and keep you alive. The shooting stopped back there when you were removed from the scene.''

She took a calming breath and steadied her voice. "So where are we going?''

"We're going to ground,'' he told her. "Find a nice quiet place. Somewhere no one would think to look for you.''

"Home?'' That sounded like a great plan to her. No one would think to look for her at the one place where she should be.

His mouth cracked into a near smile. "Not likely, Ms. Gardner. I think you've been visible enough for one day.'' He didn't look at her but swung the wheel in another fast exit. "We're going to find a sleazy little motel so we can regroup and get to know each other better.''

Sloan chuckled when he'd spotted the look of absolute terror on Lainie's face as he mentioned the sleazy motel. Her wide green eyes were filled with shock. Either she was afraid of stepping down a rung on her social ladder by checking into a fleabag joint, or she was terrified at the thought of getting to know him any better.

But for him, as he'd said the words, a picture had formed in his mind of her looking up at him from a motel bed, glistening with sweat, panting and breathless from having been completely loved—by him. Oh, and he would do a very thorough job of loving her, too. That was a pure fact. But now was not the time for those thoughts.

He forced himself to push aside the lustful images and concentrated instead on trolling the surface streets, backtracking and sidetracking to make sure the tail was gone. Trying not to think about how close she'd come to being killed, Sloan instead considered why a stalker would've hired professional killers.

That mode of operation certainly didn't fit the profile of an ordinary nutcase. Most stalkers who took the time to send a warning letter generally wanted to see the face of their intended victims when they finally made a move.

Nothing about this case added up.

He found what he'd been searching for in a run-down dump located a few blocks off Westheimer in an area that had seen better days. The End of the Trail Motel had a parking lot in back where he could pull in under overhanging trees and hopefully not be spotted.

Cutting the engine, he turned to Lainie and nearly lost his breath. The woman's sleeves were covered in blood and her hair glittered with tiny shards of glass. He wondered if he should be taking her to the nearest hospital, not to some dirty joint with peeling stucco walls and half-graveled driveways.

"You never answered me before, Lainie." His voice cracked as he tried to sound calm. "Where are you hurt? Did any of the bullets hit you?"

She shook her head. "I didn't get a chance to answer you, or even get two words in for that matter. And I'll be surprised if I'm not totally black and blue from that wild ride. But no…I don't think I was shot. I just can't imagine where all this blood came from."

"Sit quietly until I get us checked in, then. We need to make sure you're not cut and still bleeding. Try not to move too much." His heart was beating double time at the thought of leaving her alone, even for a few minutes. But he had no choice.

"Check in here? We're going to stay at this place?"

"Just long enough to figure out what to do," he told her as he stepped from the truck. "Now, be still and wait for me. Any more sudden movements and some of that glass in your hair might get in your eyes." He pushed the truck's automatic-door-lock buttons and stalked toward the motel's office.

It took her a long moment to drag in another breath. Glass in her eyes? All of a sudden she realized she was scared. Down-deep, panic-inducing scared.

She was afraid to cry, didn't even want to tremble for fear of the glass. But it wasn't the thought of being cut that had her so terrified. No. It was the idea that someone out there truly wanted to kill her.

Worse yet, she simply couldn't let herself get out of control. Oh, how she wished she had her sister here to talk to. Suzy always had an amazing way of calming her down and seeing the right answers through the haze of conflicting information. But Suzy might be fighting for her life right now. That inconceivable thought was the real reason Lainie was feeling so at a loss.

And now she would have to stay in a broken-down motel with a lawman who seemed like the strong, silent he-man type—and was gorgeous to boot.

Lordy, she was too scared to think straight. What difference did it make what Sloan looked like?

She had to start thinking clearly. She was bright enough and tough enough to outsmart any old stalker. All she had to do was concentrate on the problem and stop being sidetracked.

The truck's door locks clicked again and Sloan wrenched open the passenger side door. "Your castle awaits, ma'am."

He wouldn't let her walk the fifty feet to a room he'd already opened that faced the back lot. Swiftly and quietly he carried her toward the two-story cement building, the one painted a pea-green color.

All the while she worried about him putting his hands on her body. And wondered how in the world she was supposed to concentrate on anything else.

Gently setting her on her feet just inside the door, he shut and locked it behind them. Then he ordered her to close her eyes.

"Why?" Although the cheap motel bedspread and the spot-stained gold carpeting left a lot to be desired, she couldn't imagine what he wanted to keep her from seeing.

"Just close your eyes and be quiet a minute," he replied. "Before we do anything else, I've got to remove a few tiny bits of glass that have fallen onto your eyelashes."

"Oh." Closing her lids carefully, she decided to quit fighting and let him do what he needed to do.

Sloan opened the first-aid kit he'd taken from the back of his pickup. He ripped apart the packaging on the cotton sheeting and used it to gently pick a few slivers that had shattered onto her face and neck. As he did, he couldn't help but notice her soft, milky complexion.

Working close, he was fascinated by a faint smattering of freckles across the bridge of her nose. In his mind those slight imperfections only made her more interesting.

Trying to concentrate on the glass, he gently swiped the cotton across her thick eyelashes. Without warning, the urge to kiss the tender skin on her closed lids made him nervous and hesitant to touch her again.

He wanted to watch while she opened her eyes, focusing on his face. Sure that he would find passion in that gaze, he could already taste his growing need.

Sloan barely remembered the last time a woman affected him this way. It had been months since he'd even bothered with a date. Women just weren't a big priority in his life. Never had been. Until now.

He gritted his teeth and kept on working. When he ran the cotton over her hair, he noticed that the blood there and on her clothes had dried. If she'd been bleeding once, the flow had stopped.

Knowing she didn't need an emergency room helped to calm him down. But then he suddenly found himself fighting off the desire to dig his fingers through luscious, intense-red strands of hair. He gritted his teeth and carefully brushed the glass away instead.

"That's the best I can do," he said at last. "Do you want help getting out of your clothes?"

"Excuse me?" Her hot-green eyes popped open.

Oh, man. He desperately tried to find something else to concentrate on until he could stop imagining her naked.

"You have to get out of those things so we can check you over for cuts," he finally directed.

"I think I can handle it, thank you," she told him

with a wry smile. "But first I need to make a phone call, if you don't mind."

"No calls." He went to the phone, ripped the cord from both the wall and the phone itself and stuffed the wiring into the pocket of his heavy jacket.

"Hey!" She started toward him with a murderous look in her eyes. "What'd you do that for?"

"Who do you need to call, Lainie? A boyfriend?" That wasn't what he'd meant to ask, he chided himself. What business of his was it if she had a boyfriend?

"No. I don't have a boyfriend. I stay too busy for such things." She made a sudden move to grab his arm. "It's my sister. I have to know if Suzy is all right." A horrified look spread across her face. "I've just realized...if this isn't my blood, it must be hers. I never should've left her there."

"You didn't leave her. I took you. The shooting was directed at you, not her. With all the madhouse there, the only way to make sure no one else caught another bullet meant for you was to remove you from the scene."

Once more he searched his pockets for the mobile phone. "Take a shower and check for any nicks that might need attention. I'm going outside to phone the captain again, let him know you're not in any immediate danger. I'll ask about your sister."

Then, without really knowing why it seemed so important, Sloan searched for a way to take the fearful expression from her face and to calm the near-hysterical sound of her voice.

"Why the hell didn't you stay in your office and wait for me like you were told?" he asked with a pretend snarl. "Anyone with half a brain would know not to stand out in the open and in such a public place while they were being stalked and threatened."

That remark seemed to do what he'd intended. Instead of fear, anger sparked across Lainie's features.

She narrowed darkened emerald eyes at him and propped her hands on her hips. "So I should've cowered in my office, waiting for some big-shouldered man to come save me? Is that what you're saying?"

He'd hoped she had a temper, and it sure looked like he'd been right. The red hair was a dead give-away.

"Look, lady. From now until we catch the guy, you will do exactly as I say. No more waltzing around in plain view. I'm here to see to it you stay alive." He waited for the fire to reach her eyes again. "Now be a good girl and get those clothes off."

She took a menacing step in his direction and clenched her fists. The lights in her eyes were stunning, and for just a moment he was paralyzed with need. He should have thought of what this diversion might do to him.

Instead of hanging around, though, Sloan made a strategic retreat from the motel room. He was out of there quicker than a brushfire could burn through a parched field. And he didn't take another breath until he was in the parking lot and away from the temptation of all that passionate heat.

Not once in his entire career had he considered that he might become anyone's bodyguard. In fact, he wouldn't be doing it now except that the man he most respected in the world had asked him as a personal favor. He should be out of state, fulfilling a deathbed wish with this leave of absence from the Rangers—not baby-sitting a fiery, hot-tempered woman.

Sloan fought his reaction to the flaming lust Lainie's anger had brought out in him. Gulping down the last remnants of desire, he swore under his breath.

The assignment to protect Lainie Gardner's body might just turn out to be a lot more difficult than he'd ever imagined.

Two

Sick to her stomach and madder than all get-out, Lainie tossed a string of bad words toward the back of the motel room door as it closed behind Sloan. Being angry at him was the only way she could survive her conflicting emotions.

She hardly ever used curse words, however. And she had no idea where she'd learned a few of the ones she'd just thrown out. What was the matter with her?

Yes, she was scared beyond all reason, and near hysterical at the thought that her sister might be injured—or worse. But none of that accounted for the lust she'd felt as Sloan stood there with that teasing grin on his face. The flashes of heat and weakness his look created pushed pure old-fashioned desire trembling down her spine. The anger had actually turned her on.

She was mad again just thinking about it. How stupid could one supposedly smart woman be?

Her shakes started once more. She felt them move up her wobbly legs and spread across her body. Good grief.

Was her body betraying her need for Sloan? She prayed that her reaction to him was just some weird kind of delayed stress related to her crazy predicament.

Desperately wanting to regain the control and determination she'd become famous for, Lainie fought her own emotions. She was always in charge of every situation and this one should be no different. The danger was over. It was time to start thinking instead of feeling.

And all she could think of was the arousal in Sloan's chestnut-colored eyes as he'd headed out the door? Oh dear Lord, help her. The stress must be driving her totally insane.

Lainie wasn't the kind of woman who was normally disgusted by the thought of good healthy sex. Far from it. She'd had a couple of great experiences with that very thing in her checkered youth. But that was long ago. Besides that, she simply did not jump into bed with total strangers—not even ones who'd just saved her life.

Struggling to even out her ragged breathing, she ordered herself to stop all this idiotic emotional stuff and to start thinking. Just close her eyes, clear her mind and rationally consider her options.

When she finally managed to close her eyes for a few seconds, they popped right back open as the shaking began again. Instead of waiting for the trembling to stop this time, she focused on her surroundings, and the reality of the room hit her with a sickening rush. It stopped the shakes but gave her a headache instead. What a truly awful place to pick to hide.

Using her vivid imagination, she could tell that forty or fifty years ago these furnishings might've been someone's idea of fashionable. The avocado walls, gold carpeting and dreadful flower-print bedspread looked as if they'd seen much better days.

A cheap chair, a metal rack with two wire hangers and a TV set with an old-fashioned rabbit-ears antenna were the only items besides the bed in this cramped room. The place smelled of stale cigarettes. And the heavy rubber-backed drapes over the one lone window contributed to a depressing atmosphere.

Lainie checked the bathroom and found two plastic cups wrapped in little paper jackets, a green-glass ashtray and the smallest bar of soap she'd ever seen. All of it had been crammed onto the edge of a single cracked sink.

Two yellowed towels sat folded on the back of the toilet, while the plastic shower curtain hung crookedly off its metal rings. Boy oh boy. The lap of luxury.

As much as she hated the thought of stripping down in this joint, she hated the idea of having glass slivers embedded in her skin even more. With a careful sigh, Lainie grabbed a towel and fitted it over her hair. The tiny thing wasn't big enough to cover her head, but it would have to do while she took off her clothes and stepped into the shower.

Sloan balanced the two soda cans in one hand while he pulled the motel room key from his pocket with the other. He carefully inserted the key in the lock and waited for either the chain to stop him or for a heavy object to come flying at his head. Neither thing happened, so he pushed the door open and walked into the room.

He'd given her a full half hour, hoping that she'd use the time to calm down and take a shower. Actually, the idea of a cold shower had sounded pretty good to him when he'd last walked out of here.

The bathroom door stood ajar and he could hear the water running. Guess she'd decided a long, cold shower was just what she'd needed, too.

"Lainie! It's me," he called out, hoping not to frighten her.

"Wait. Hold on."

After a few seconds the water stopped. She appeared in the bathroom doorway. And suddenly he couldn't have moved if his life depended upon it.

Her hair had darkened with wetness and hung down to her shoulders, dripping water over her bare skin—all of that totally naked, glistening skin.

She'd apparently just stepped out of the shower, because she stood there looking up at him with an exasperated look on her face. And nothing to cover her nakedness except a postage-stamp-size towel that she was trying to spread out over her important parts.

He let his gaze shoot down her body to the long, slender legs and nearly bit his tongue. Dang, but he'd surely love to be able to touch all that soft skin. It was everything he could do just to drag his eyes back up to meet hers.

"Uh…" he stuttered. "Sorry. I thought you'd be

out of the shower long ago. I can go away and come back in later.'' That was…if he could force his legs to propel him out the door.

Lainie shook her head. "It won't help. My clothes had so many specks of glass that I decided to rinse them out in the tub." The edge of the towel slipped as she talked and she was forced to hang on with both hands. "But I've just realized that it'll be tomorrow before they're dry enough to put back on. What am I going to do?''

He could think of about a half-dozen things that she could do while she waited. And every single one of them involved him—and most of them involved the bed.

But she looked so forlorn, so annoyed with herself, that he felt a grin coming on. Sloan opened his mouth to make a smart remark but the irritated look in her eyes pulled him up short. She was the subject of his mission, not the object of his desire. And he'd better start treating her that way.

"Did you try wrapping up in the bedspread?''

She narrowed her eyes at him. "It's too heavy. I couldn't walk with it around me. Think of something else.''

"I have a raincoat out in the truck that'll cover you up. It won't be high fashion, but I suppose it'll do.''

For a second he got lost in those startling green eyes again. He wondered if he could make them turn as dark as they'd been when she'd been so angry before. Would passion turn them that same depthless color?

"Yes, a raincoat would be great. Thanks." Her glittering eyes scrunched up in thought. "What did you find out about my sister?'' she demanded, dragging him back to earth with a thunk.

''Captain Johnson says she's been taken to the hospital. He knows she's going to be all right, but he isn't sure how badly she's been hurt. He'll check it out and get back to us later.''

''Okay.'' Lainie's breath hitched as though she'd cut off a little sob. ''She's really going to be okay? Thank God.''

Lainie looked so forlorn and anguished standing there with nothing on and water dripping off her hair. The sight of her like that did things to him that he didn't understand. It wasn't pure lust, but what it really was eluded him at the moment.

He turned to leave, then looked down at the cans in his hands. ''Are you thirsty? I brought you a soda,'' he told her as he turned back.

''Oh, yes, please.'' Her voice was tentative and her eyes still held that haunted look.

For one brief second he considered taking her in his arms and giving her all the protection and comfort she so obviously needed. But that wouldn't be professional. And right now he desperately needed to maintain an air of professionalism.

Dignity. That's what the situation called for. *Remember the Rangers. Remember duty.*

Sloan set both cans on the bed and was back out the door before she could move her first muscle. He retrieved his old black raincoat from the pickup and then counted to one hundred. Not that he needed the time to gather his wits. No indeed. He'd simply wanted to give her back a little of her own dignity for a few minutes.

When he finally reentered the room, he found that

she'd left the bathroom door cracked open a few inches and was nowhere to be seen. Smart lady.

"Here's the coat," he mumbled. He shoved the raincoat through the opening while he turned his head away.

He felt her grab for it and then heard the door slam shut. One minute later Lainie sauntered out.

The beat-up old duster had never looked so good. It usually hit him at about knee length, but on her it dangled just above the ankles. She'd buttoned it up all the way and had the belt snugly tied around her middle.

"Thanks again. That's better," she said as she rolled up the sleeves. "And thanks for the soda, too. I didn't realize how dry my throat was."

"You're welcome. Are you hungry? There's a café a half mile down the road that we can take a chance on if you'd like." He hadn't given any consideration to her comfort since this whole thing began.

Some bodyguard he made. Her physical needs were every bit as important to her survival as was keeping her safe from outside threats. Starving both of them wouldn't exactly get him a commendation from the captain.

Instead of answering him, Lainie covered her face with her hand. "I can't think of food," she moaned, and plopped down on the bed. "I can't think of anything but Suzy. What have I done to my sister?"

He couldn't bear to see such a strong, competent woman dissolve like this. Sitting down beside her, he slid an arm around her shoulders and drew her close.

"I told you before, you didn't do any of this. You

weren't the one aiming bullets toward a lobby full of people. I doubt that you wanted any of this to happen. Did you?''

She glanced up at him with a wretched look of self-pity in her eyes. "No, of course not. But I should've paid more attention to the threats. I should've waited in my office for you to arrive. It's my fault that she was standing next to me in front of those windows.''

The guilt he heard when she spoke nearly did him in. "Easy, there. Life can be chock-full of should'ves, you know. Blaming yourself is useless. It won't bring you any peace or change the outcome one bit. And it only buys you more heartache.''

Lainie heard the pain in the quiet tone of Sloan's voice. It made her wonder what had happened in his life that he would change if only he had a second chance.

She gazed into his eyes just in time to catch the sad look he quickly hid again. He'd never talk to her about his troubles, she knew. But that was what she did for a living. Listening and giving advice.

Deciding not to ask any personal questions until she knew him better, Lainie moved out of his embrace. "Can I see Suzy? Will you take me to the hospital?''

He slowly shook his head. "Sorry. The captain said for us to lay low tonight. Even if we knew where they'd taken your sister, it would be too risky. The hospital would be too open, too predictable.''

"You mean someone might try to kill me there? This…this person would be at the hospital waiting for us?''

"It's a possibility.''

"Who did this? Who wanted to hurt me this badly?"

"Both of those are great questions," he told her as he stood and stretched. "Can we discuss them while we're getting something to eat?"

She bit back sudden irritation. After all, he wasn't a family member who cared what she thought. He was merely her bodyguard. She didn't mean anything to him, so why should he help her figure out who the stalker might be?

"Okay," she agreed finally. "I guess I could choke down a salad."

He raised an eyebrow at her and let his gaze slowly wander from her soaking-wet hair all the way down to her bare feet.

"We'll be on foot. We can't take a chance of being spotted in the truck tonight. So you'd better put on your shoes, Ms. Gardner." The grin broke out across his face again. "But don't count on a salad in this part of town. You're probably going to have to settle for a burger."

A half hour later Lainie sat huddled with his raincoat pulled tightly around her. Her feet, stuffed into two-inch heels with no nylons, were neatly stashed under a plastic-covered booth in a dimly lit Mexican café.

She was trying to decide whether to order a taco salad or a plate of enchiladas. She'd already gulped down a tall glass of sweetened iced tea and was just about to polish off an entire basketful of tortilla chips.

"I thought you wanted a salad?" Sloan grumbled from his spot across the table. "We walked two extra blocks out of our way to find this place. Just order the salad and be done with it.''

He'd already placed his order with the waitress. Now, looking rather impatient, he waited for her to make a decision.

Lainie dipped the last chip into the tomato salsa and ordered the enchiladas. Since Captain Johnson returned their call to say that Suzy was still in the hospital but in good condition, Lainie's appetite had returned with a vengeance.

Sloan relaxed back against the faded-brown bench and flipped his hat onto the seat next to him. The dim lighting in the restaurant didn't afford much of a view, but she could manage to see that his hair was the same color as his eyes. A warm brown with golden highlights, it was neatly cut, but one stray strand hung down across his forehead.

He brushed back the wayward hair, and Lainie cautioned herself not to sigh aloud. She wondered whether it would feel as soft and silky as the mink coat it resembled. She managed to blink away the questions.

''We've got ourselves a problem here,'' Sloan drawled.

Lainie wondered if he realized exactly how big a problem it was for her every time he smiled, and she found herself yearning to place a kiss on the dimple in his chin.

''You mean something other than dodging bullets from the sniper's gun?'' she asked, instead of saying what she thought.

''You've got a smart mouth, you know that?'' He grinned and took a swig from the long-neck beer bottle that the waitress had just put in front of him.

"Well, excuse me, but I'm not exactly feeling too polite at the moment. I'm tired and irritable. My sister is in the hospital because of me. And I'm sitting here in a heavy raincoat that's so big it's falling off my shoulders, wondering whether this may be my last meal." Her eyes glittered with sparkling green anger.

Sloan thought she was really something special. What other woman would react to being shot at by becoming mad and irritable? He knew most of them would've dissolved into a quivering mass of nervous hysterics by now.

But he wasn't about to mention his admiration to Lainie. "Things could be worse," he mumbled.

"Oh, really?"

He looked past her to the picture of a bullfighter on the wall. "At least you have people who are worried about you and who would care if you lived or died."

She opened her mouth to make a remark, but the waitress brought the food just then. Before the plates could be arranged on the table in front of them, they both dug in without another word.

It wasn't long until Sloan polished off the last flour tortilla and signaled the waitress to bring another beer. "You're not going to be able to go back home for a while, you know."

Her eyes widened and she swallowed her last bite of food with a cough. "What? Why not?"

"It won't be possible to provide you with adequate protection if you just go blithely back to your old routine. After you give your statement to the police detectives, you and I will have to disappear." He watched as she picked up her fork and squeezed her fingers in a death grip around the handle. "This might be a good time to consider a mini vacation. Someplace where no one will recognize your face."

"I have to work. With my sister in the hospital, someone needs to do the columns. I have contracts to fulfill and people who are desperate for my advice."

"Your sister writes the columns?"

"I give the advice, she makes sure it appears in the column the way I intended."

"I heard somewhere that columnists usually have a couple of weeks worth of columns stashed away for emergencies. What if you were taken ill or had to take some time off for other personal reasons?"

She slid down on the booth's bench. "I do have a few backup columns. But still, without Suzy I will have to make sure they get turned in and are set the way we expect them to be."

"Could you give someone else instructions on where to find your files and then check to make sure it's done properly by using a computer and the Internet?"

She grimaced, heaving a sigh. "I suppose. But..."

"Great. One problem solved," he interrupted. "We'll have the captain rig up a laptop for us, and he can send a secretary to your office for your files." He tipped his beer for a fast sip before he quickly plowed ahead. "Now, the next problem is finding a place to hide out."

"If this is a vacation, why don't we just go to a five-star resort somewhere?" she asked as she munched on the tip of her iced tea straw. "I've been meaning to try that new place I've heard so much about on the Big Island in Hawaii. Why don't we go there?''

He stopped the chuckle before it escaped his lips. ''I don't think Captain Johnson would be able to afford it, for one thing. And for another, we need to find a place where no one will recognize you, remember?'' He was trying to keep the fear out of her eyes.

She ignored his question and honed in on the cost. ''Why would Captain Johnson have to pay for it? I've got money. We can just put it on my credit card.''

Sloan shook his head and tried to keep the exasperated expression from his face. ''Well, that might make some sense…*if* you had your wallet and credit cards with you. And if—''

''My purse! I forgot I dropped my purse when the shooting started.'' The panicked look was back in her eyes.

''Don't worry,'' he told her. ''I'm sure the detectives have found it by now. And you can't use the cards, anyway. Credit card charges are one of the easiest things to trace. From now on we're strictly on a cash basis.''

Her eyes clouded over and he was fascinated by the muddy-river green color they had become. But she didn't seem to have much else to say on the subject of how they paid for their getaway. He was grateful he'd remembered to bring along a few hundred in cash.

''One of my buddies in the Rangers has a cabin somewhere in the hill country,'' Sloan mentioned, trying to sound casual. ''He's got it up for sale, but I don't think he'd mind if we used it for a few days.

What do you think?'' He knew she must be feeling as if her world had tilted on its axis.

"I suppose so.'' Lainie sounded so tentative that Sloan wanted to find a way to put the strength back in her voice.

"I'll call him later and arrange it. Meanwhile…'' Sloan hesitated, but in the end decided that even her anger had been better than this forlorn look. "Let's go on back to our room and get some sleep.''

"*Our* room?'' she yelped. "You think we're both going to sleep in that tiny cubbyhole? Fat chance, buster.''

A flashdance of anger burned in her eyes, and Sloan breathed a silent sigh of relief that the spark was back. "Well, tell you what, sweetheart. If you don't want to stay there, and since you don't have any cash on you, I'll be glad to give you the use of my truck for the night.

"The passenger seat reclines,'' he continued as he covertly surveyed her reactions. "It shouldn't be too uncomfortable for one night. But it might turn cold later on. Sure hope you don't freeze.''

It was a thrill to see the bright pink flush of frustration spread across her features. She straightened her back and scowled.

So what if that look could burn a hole right through a steel door? At least her spirit was intact.

Her eyes narrowed to little slits when he didn't make any other remarks and simply flagged the waitress to request the bill.

"All right,'' she grumbled. "We can both stay in that little cave if you insist. But you'd better be praying that the bathtub is more comfortable than it looks, cause that's where you're headed. There's no chance in the world that we're both going to be sleeping in the same bed tonight.''

Three

———

"So what's your plan for the night?" Lainie asked. They'd just locked themselves firmly inside the cheap motel room once again. "Where do you intend to sleep?"

Sloan sat down and stretched out companionably on the double bed, his body fully extended and his head propped up against the wall behind it. "The bed isn't half-bad." He patted the narrow spot next to him. "Try it out for yourself."

The look on her face was priceless, Sloan mused. He loved it when he got to her, and he wondered why that was.

Since she continued to stand there, staring down at the ugly bedspread as if it were a rattler pit, he decided to try a different tack. "Look. It's early yet. Why don't you sit and tell me about your job? Maybe together we can come up with a reason why someone wants to kill you.'' He pushed the lone pillow up against the wall for her.

When she tentatively checked to make sure the top button of his raincoat was securely fastened at her neck before she sat on the bed, it was all Sloan could do to keep a straight face. But he refused to laugh. He was feeling unsure enough about his own motives, let alone hers.

She settled in as far away from him as physically possible. ''Maybe you're right. I'm still too tense to sleep, anyway.''

He allowed himself a half smile, while she took off her shoes and daintily dropped them on the floor.

''Okay.'' She wiggled her bottom down into the mattress until she'd apparently nestled herself into a more comfortable position. ''That's better. What do you want to know?''

''Well,'' he began as he toed his boots off, ''I thought maybe you'd just start talking. You know, tell me about how a normal day goes, what kind of letters you receive, that sort of thing.'' He reached over, wanting to flick a tiny, lingering crumb off her chin, but quickly caught himself.

''Oh, but that's so boring,'' she sighed. ''Are you sure hearing about that stuff might help?''

He shrugged a shoulder. ''You never know. What else have we got to do?''

The minute he said it, the visions of what else he'd like to be doing in this bed blindsided him. But if Lainie noticed the change, she didn't mention it.

''My day always starts at six-thirty. Suzy and I jog every morning. It gets the blood moving.''

''Your sister lives with you?'' He eased his body around slightly and tried to concentrate on her words, but shifting his focus didn't do much to change the tension.

She looked startled for a second. "Oh, that's right. You don't know about my family."

"Captain Johnson just told me that you were a single woman and that your mother was a longtime, dear friend of his. I assumed you either lived alone or with your mother."

Lainie smiled then and folded her hands in her lap. "I sort of do both…live alone and also live with my family, that is. A few years back, I bought a big house in a fancy Houston suburb. It's an old place and has a good-size guest house right on the grounds. I bought it with the idea in mind of letting my sister and her husband use the guest house."

She frowned at a large crack in the wall directly in front of the bed. "But when it came time for us to move in, I realized that the two of them would be much more comfortable in the bigger place. So…"

"You moved into the guest house," he said with a yawn.

"Yes, but it wasn't a hardship. The smaller house is so cozy. It's just perfect for my needs. And Jeff, he's my brother-in-law, loves to entertain and have big parties. Someday, the two of them might have a bunch of kids, too, and the living arrangements have all worked out for the best. Without family nearby, a person is no one."

"But you own both houses?"

"Sure. In fact, a year or so ago I bought a neighboring house when the old woman who lived there passed away. It was a good thing, too. My father had a stroke a few months later, so I insisted that he and Mom move in next door so I could keep an eye on them." She inclined her head. "I suppose you could say we live in a family compound."

Sloan could not imagine anything worse. The thought of having people—meddling family members especially—underfoot all the time gave him the creeps.

"Sounds real cozy," he said, using her words and with a grin he didn't feel. "So your father is still alive. Does he work?"

"He's totally disabled. Confined to a wheelchair," she said sadly.

"And your brother-in-law…what does he do for a living?"

Lainie studied her toes. "Well, Jeff runs my father's bar now. It's not much of a living, though. The place is only open a few hours a day, except on weekends. Mom keeps the books, but it never has been much of a moneymaker."

Sloan got the picture. Lainie seemed to be the sole support for the whole clan. He wondered if she realized how much friction could arise between family members when one strong person ruled the purse strings. As a lawman he'd seen that kind of thing happen often enough.

"Hmm. Let me get this straight in my head," he began. "All of your immediate family lives in housing that you own and no doubt provide free of charge."

"I couldn't ask my family to pay me."

"Uh-huh. And you are the one person in the family who is gainfully employed."

"My sister works hard in her job at the paper."

"I'm sure she does. But you're her boss, right?"

"Yes, but—"

"So without you, what would become of the rest of the family?"

Those great green eyes widened and she twisted the edge of the bedspread around in her fingers. "I've provided for them in my will, of course. And I imagine that Suzy could keep the column going for quite a while if I were ill. I've been letting her write a few of the columns so she could get the practice."

"Seems to me that the whole bunch of them ought to be real concerned over your welfare."

"That's not fair." She stood up and began pacing from the bed to the door and back. "They're my family. All families have a few problems, but that doesn't mean they don't love each other." She stopped and held her palm out, pleading for him to understand. "You must know how it is. Family is the most important thing in the world. You probably have a few family problems of your own. Everyone does."

His silence told Lainie a lot about the man. There was something about his family that bothered him.

Finally he shook his head. "Don't have a family," he muttered.

"None? No wife…or ex-wife…and kids?"

He scowled. "Never been married."

"But surely you must have parents. Were you orphaned at an early age or something?" She sat down on the edge of the bed and studied him again.

"Nope. Had a mother…up until December fifteenth."

"Your mother just passed away three months ago?" She gulped, wondering how she'd gotten herself into such a stupid conversation in the first place. "I'm so sorry, Sloan. Were you two very close?"

His eyes turned dark and he looked away. "Not really. I didn't get back to visit her much. It'd been maybe six years or so since the last time."

From the sound of his voice, she wondered if he'd even had a chance to speak to his mother before her death. In her typical prying way, Lainie couldn't stand not asking.

"Uh…maybe this isn't any of my business, but were you two estranged over something? Many of my advice columns touch on the guilt people feel after the death of a family member. The worst is when they'd never gotten the chance to reconcile their problems, and all of a sudden it's too late."

It was Sloan's turn to stand. He took off the denim jacket, and for the first time Lainie saw the gun stuck in a holster at his waistband. The sight of it put a cold damper on the hot lust she'd begun to feel at the sight of his tight, muscular butt encased in superslim jeans.

"You're right," he said over his shoulder as he hung up the jacket and unknotted his tie. "It's none of your business."

That put her in her place. She should've known better than to try to befriend an uptight, close-mouthed lawman. Well, fine.

"I have an overnight kit in the truck," he told her as he removed the holster and checked the gun. "Do you want me to rustle up some toothpaste and stuff for you to use? You could sleep in one of my T-shirts, if you like. That would probably be more comfortable than the heavy old raincoat." He pulled off the Ranger's badge and laid it down on top of the television with his gun.

"I'm not sleeping with you," she huffed. "Not in anything."

"Suit yourself." He undid his belt, pulled it through the loops and hung it over the metal rod. "Mind if I turn on the TV, then? I sleep better with a little noise."

"You can honestly think of sleeping at a time like this?"

"I'm tired. You'd be smart to try catching a few zees yourself." His voice was edgy and not at all as sexy as it had been earlier. "You've got a big day tomorrow," he continued as he flipped on the set and sat back down on his side of the bed.

She folded her arms over her chest and prepared to tell him exactly what she expected of him tomorrow. But for a second she was distracted by the local news and the eerie pictures of her office building with the front lobby windows blown out.

When she turned back to say something, he was already out cold. She couldn't believe he'd become unconscious that fast. He'd better not snore.

Lainie got up and went to the bathroom, flipping off the overhead light on her way. When she was done, she left the bathroom door slightly ajar so the light in there could act as a nightlight.

She settled back down on her edge of the tiny bed and prayed the big lummox sleeping next to her didn't roll around in his sleep. She'd hate to have to fight him off during the night. And there was no place else in the room for her to watch TV.

Frowning at the screen, where a late-night talk-show host was beginning his stand-up routine, she tried to ignore Sloan's reclining body while she considered her options. The trouble was, she didn't seem to have any options at all.

The longer she fumed over her predicament, the heavier her eyelids became. But she wasn't going to lose control and fall asleep. No way. She intended to stay up, watching TV and keeping an eye on the very masculine body in her bed.

Sloan woke up with a cramp in his shoulder. He tried to move, but found himself wrapped up in long legs and soft female curves. Lainie's head rested comfortably against his shoulder, and her peaceful expression in repose seemed a little too quiet, a little too angelic to suit him.

He took a breath and smelled woman, musty raincoat and a hint of soap. Her languid, slow breathing was intimate, familiar. Yet it was not at all like anything he'd ever shared with anyone.

He'd never slept all night with a woman before. The morning-after routine had always sounded too nerve-racking and embarrassing for his style. Why mess up a night of pleasure with the aggravation of trying to find a polite way out?

But there was just something about sleeping with Lainie that soothed him. Who would've guessed that an annoying yet lust-inspiring woman would be the one to make him feel all comfortable and homey?

Before he thought about it too much, Sloan brushed his hand over her sleep-tousled hair, pushing it back behind her ear. Deep-red silk. The satiny-soft feel of her seemed in stark contrast to the strong spirit and sexy brashness he knew she possessed.

His blood stirred and he had to remind himself

that she was under his protection. She was quite a woman—a family-loving, advice-giving dream girl. And it was too damned bad that they hadn't met at another time.

Speaking of time, Sloan glanced at his watch and realized that dawn was near. Time to check in with the captain and finalize plans to hide this erotic and baffling female.

He inched out from under her and then stood beside the bed, watching as she shifted around trying to get comfortable. She rolled onto her back. A few of the buttons on his old raincoat had pulled loose during the night and patches of creamy skin appeared at both her chest and thigh.

The restless, uncivilized beast in him growled at the sight. He fought to remember his normal reserves. Repeating a couple of Ranger slogans about standards and duty, Sloan backed away from the bed.

Needing a little distance and a lot more fortitude than he was feeling at the moment, Sloan retrieved his kit from the car, then went into the bathroom to strip and step into the tepid shower.

In her dream, Lainie was standing alone in the frigid rain. The water dripped off her hair, trickling down her back. A steamy, cool mist fogged her vision.

A man was out there in the fog. A man she couldn't see but knew wanted to kill her. Searching for a place to hide, she had the distinct impression that the shadowy figure who stalked her was someone she knew.

''Don't try to hide, Lainie,'' a low voice whispered.

Who could this be? The voice was achingly familiar. She racked her brain for answers.

Perhaps it was someone from work. But why would anyone there wish her harm? A chill ran down her back, and she felt the goose bumps rising on her arms, but she set her jaw and stood her ground.

Her time was running short. Through the mist she could feel his hot breath on the back of her neck.

She shoved out at the fog and tried to see where her assailant might be. With no warning, Sloan appeared beside her. Sloan? No. It was not possible.

Blinded and frightened, she turned away from him and ran. He called out, and she felt a sudden thud in her left shoulder.

Lainie came awake with the blood still pounding in her chest. ''What? Where…?''

Sloan was shaking her shoulder. ''Time to get up. I just talked to Captain Johnson.''

She finally woke up enough to recognize Sloan. But the minute she saw his eyes, she managed to pull herself together in time to shake off the vestiges of sleep and wipe the nightmare images from her mind. Sloan might be infuriating and demanding, but he was definitely not a threat to her.

Unless you counted him as a threat to her heart. And maybe that's exactly what her dream was trying to tell her.

She was positive her stalker was not the Texas Ranger. But she promised herself that later she'd work on figuring out who might really want to hurt her. The scary dream had to be some kind of warning or clue, and she wished Suzy was here to help her decipher it.

"Wow…I just had a doozy of a dream," she told him as she swallowed past the tremors still causing her to stutter.

He ignored what she said and handed her a paper cup filled with coffee. "Sorry to wake you, but we've got places to go and things to do."

"Really?" She drank a swig of coffee and immediately felt better, human. "Where are we going?"

"To a nearby police substation. Captain Johnson will be there to meet us. We both need to file witness reports on the shooting yesterday."

Lainie stood and stretched, arching her back like a lazy cat. It was a picture Sloan could've done without.

It was bad enough that, because she was groggy, she seemed limp and pliable and sexy as all get-out. Her hair was messed up by the ravages of a nightmare and her lids were still half-closed in what could only be described as bedroom eyes.

"Go put your clothes on," he grumbled. "I just checked and they're dry."

She obeyed his command with no comment, but a few minutes later she appeared at the bathroom door, dressed and back to her old self. "You didn't ask about my dream. You were in it and the whole thing was really weird." Her hand was fisted against her hip and she looked ready for a fight.

"No time for that now." He quickly slid his gun into the hidden holster under his coat. "Maybe later."

"Right, boss," she muttered. "You really are full of yourself, you know that?"

He grabbed her coat with one hand and her elbow with the other and, determined not to utter another word, hustled them both out the motel room door and into the truck.

Sloan cruised the streets, taking an out-of-the-way route to the station. When they arrived, he drove around the block six times, coming at it from different directions. He checked all the parked cars and every pedestrian.

At this point, he refused to take any chances with her life. It didn't seem logical that someone would risk taking a potshot at her while she was with the police. But then again, nothing seemed logical about this whole thing.

The police station was located in an area of town that was unfamiliar. But the station itself was built like most of the others in the metropolitan sections of Harris County. He pulled into the back lot and parked his truck in a visitor's spot. With the special plates and the regulation sticker on his windshield, Sloan knew he wouldn't be hassled there and the spot would be totally out of a potential sniper's line of sight.

He rushed Lainie from the truck and into the station. A few discreet questions later and they were directed into a conference room in the back.

"Good to see you two." Captain Johnson greeted them with a cup of coffee and a smile. "Lainie, your mother sends her love and says to tell you that everyone is okay. Suzy's wound was clean and she should be back out of the hospital in a day or two.

Oh, and I'm supposed to tell you not to worry about anything at home.''

Sloan watched while Lainie hugged the rugged and stoic captain. Her eyes filled up with tears, but she managed to hold them off. She set her shoulders and raised her chin.

The captain introduced them to a police detective who asked to interview them separately. Sloan walked to a break room with Captain Johnson while Lainie stayed to give the detective her statement.

"So, do you have a plan drawn up to protect her, son?"

Sloan nodded and sat down at the old folding table that looked as if it had seen break room duty for the last twenty years. "I contacted Sergeant Hernandez this morning, sir. His cabin on the Guadalupe near Sequin still has the electric hooked up so the real estate agents can show it. He said we're welcome to use it.''

"Lainie isn't going to like being kept away from her family and her job for too long.''

Sloan raised his eyebrow and scowled. "I can see that. Sometimes it seems she believes she's invincible…as if she's wrapped in an acrylic barrier and can't be hurt. It's kind of weird.''

The captain put his hand on his shoulder. "I've known Lainie since she was born. She's a genius and absolutely brilliant at her job. But she has devoted so much time to her work and giving advice to others that she's rather naive about her own world.

"And her family does everything possible to keep her that way," the captain continued. "They've always protected her from anything harmful. They're absolutely convinced that she needs to feel safe and secure to do her job.''

"But this stalker is obviously a real threat,'' Sloan interjected. "I tried to make light of it by asking her to think of this time as a mini vacation because I didn't like the look of panic in her eyes. It turned out she was a lot more concerned about her sister than her own safety.''

Captain Johnson smiled. "That's just like her. And her family and I would appreciate it if you'd do everything in your power to keep her feeling safe. Don't force her to face the real danger. After nearly thirty years of thinking she has complete control over her own destiny, we're not sure how she would react to having her secure little world crumble around her.''

Sloan wondered if perhaps he'd guessed this about her, and that was why he felt so protective of a woman who seemed so demanding. His own feelings would have to be buried. Doing a favor for his captain and protecting Lainie were the most important things.

"I'll do my best,'' he told his boss. And he meant every word.

"We're trying to keep her involvement in the shooting out of the news. The police are calling it a random act of violence since no one was killed.''

"But the police don't buy that themselves, do they?''

The captain shook his head. "They've opened a case investigation and have assigned this detective full time. He has copies of all the letters Lainie received over the last six months, as well as the original threatening e-mails and notes. The newspaper has cooperated fully.''

''Do they have some way to keep her columns appearing on a daily basis, even though neither she nor her sister will be there to file them?''

''I'll take care of that. Don't worry. You're going to have your hands full just convincing her to stay out of sight and lay low for a while.''

''Not a problem, Captain.'' Sloan took a swig of cold coffee and swallowed hard. ''Sir? Do you think this feels like a normal stalker situation? It doesn't seem to fit the regular profiles.''

Captain Johnson raised both brows and smiled. ''Can't keep you out of the investigation, can I?''

Sloan winced, wishing he would've kept his mouth shut. He had a personal investigation of his own that he should be attending to. But that didn't matter right now. Sloan wanted to do whatever his captain asked.

''It's all right, Sergeant. I appreciate you sticking around for this before you take your leave,'' Captain Johnson said as if he'd read his mind.

''I owe you, Captain. If it wasn't for you, I might not have entered law enforcement in the first place. And the law is the best thing that ever happened in my life. This assignment is just one small payback.''

The captain laid a hand on his shoulder and lowered his voice. ''For what it's worth, I agree that Lainie's threat is probably not coming from a typical stalker. Your main assignment here is to keep her alive, Sloan.

''Lainie's mother was my first love,'' the captain continued. ''She means a lot to me. I've promised her that we'll get Lainie's stalker before anyone else gets hurt. And I never go back on a promise."

Sloan was sure that was a true statement. And it deepened his resolve to protect Lainie's life with all the resources in his power.

He just wished Lainie wasn't quite so sexy. Or so irritatingly bossy. Maybe he should've been wishing that he could find a way not to notice so much.

After being escorted into the break room, Lainie sat down next to Captain Johnson and waited until Sloan left the room accompanying the detective. She'd been interviewed for a mere hour, but she felt exhausted and wanted a nap.

Hmm. Food first, and then a nap.

"Oh, man, am I tired." She laid her forehead against the slick tabletop and sighed.

"I know, honey." Captain Johnson patted her on the back. "What can I do for you?"

"Food. No, I take that back." She lifted her head and smiled wearily. "Chocolate…coffee…and then I want to go home."

"Sorry. I can get you a candy bar and coffee, but you can't go home just yet." Captain Johnson put a few coins into one of the vending machines against the wall that Lainie hadn't noticed when she came into the room.

After she took her first bite of a gooey chocolate bar, she managed a smile for her mother's old friend. "I want to thank you for everything, Captain. As much as Sloan Abbott is an arrogant jerk, he also managed to save my life. I don't know where I'd be without him.

"I'm so glad you insisted on me having a bodyguard," she admitted. "I just wish it hadn't been Sloan."

Chet laid a hand over her free one on the table. "I think you might want to cut him a little slack, honey. Personal security is not his regular duty. The sergeant is one of the Rangers' best crime investigators. In fact, he's the youngest man in Ranger history to receive a commendation from the governor."

Oh, right, she thought. Of course Sloan would be some kind of rising star in the Rangers.

"Besides," he continued. "I couldn't spare anyone else. The sergeant is supposed to be beginning an indefinite personal leave from the Rangers. He's the only one free."

"He's taking a leave? What for?"

The captain smiled and leaned back in his chair. "I think you'd better ask him that."

"I'd rather not," she huffed. "I need to be at home. This whole thing seems to be getting out of hand. I can't really still be in danger, can I?"

Chet shook his head and chuckled. "Leave the investigation to the professionals, Lainie. You just have to do what Sergeant Abbott tells you. And I'm afraid that means you'll have to hide out for a while."

She hated the idea of being stuck with Sloan but there was no way around it. It was a royal pain being around a man who was arrogant and withdrawn—and so gorgeous he made her knees go weak just looking at him.

An hour later Sloan loaded up his truck with the two suitcases and a duffel bag that Captain Johnson had brought for Lainie. As he hefted them into the bed, he wondered why it seemed as if her mother packed everything Lainie owned. They weren't going to be gone that long.

Earlier, Captain Johnson had slipped him a packet with $1,000 in twenties. Along with that, he'd given Sloan instructions to check in every few hours but to keep Lainie hidden until he could put together a list of suspects.

Until then, everyone—including her friends, co-workers and family—were potential suspects.

Lainie bade goodbye to the captain and silently stepped up into the passenger seat. Sloan figured this was the beginning of a very long and very tense few days.

"Buckle up," he growled as he turned the key in the ignition and the truck roared to life.

She grimaced but did as he'd ordered.

The next couple of minutes were every bit as tense and silent as he'd feared. The situation was impossible. How could he protect her if they were constantly at odds? They were going to have to find a way to get along.

"We'll be stopping for breakfast on down the road a piece," he told her, hoping that she'd see that all he wanted was her comfort and safety. "I want to be sure we aren't being followed first. Can you wait?"

"Look. We have to stay together for a few days, but I don't have to like it…and you don't have to try to be nice to me, either. I'm not hungry." She stared out her window and folded her arms over her chest.

The irritation hit him hard in the gut. "You have to eat, Lainie. We'll stop when I say we stop." Annoying woman. He wasn't about to let her starve on his watch.

"Stop if you want. I didn't realize I was your prisoner." She swiveled around to glare at him. "I thought you said to think of this as a mini vacation." The heated sparks from her flashing green eyes could've burned down the entire city of Houston.

Heat and fury crawled up his neck. He admired her backbone, but he was damned if he would put up with her controlling behavior. Their lives were at stake, dang it!

He pulled over to the side of the road, out of the traffic, and jammed the truck into park. She narrowed her eyes at him but said nothing.

Want. Need. Anger. Desire. The combination of emotions drove him over an edge he'd been careful to avoid.

He lost all control when, after unbuckling his seat belt and scooting closer to her, she grimaced and inched back. Sloan grabbed her, vised her chin in his hand and jerked her face closer to his with one swift movement.

"Listen, Ms. Gardner. You do what I say or we'll both end up dead. Got that?"

She'd managed to drive him totally nuts. And his next move proved the point.

Four

Sloan's razor-edged gaze sliced into hers. The danger she saw there was almost frightening. But the first tender touch of his hand to her face took all the fight right out of her. If it hadn't been for the instant shot of adrenaline speeding through her veins and making every nerve ending hypersensitive, Lainie's earlier temper tantrum would've been the ultimate embarrassment.

She'd rather not look like a spoiled child to Sloan. But as he continued to touch her, she froze, unable to move or think, absolutely mesmerized by the desperation she recognized in his deep-brown eyes.

For several tense seconds, Sloan scanned her face. He seemed to be calculating his next move. Before she had a chance to gather her senses enough to wriggle away from him, his fingers loosened their grip on her chin and he began stroking her cheek.

The silky sensations he was creating on her face started to drive tingles to other places in her body. He combed his fingers through her hair, eventually cupping the back of her head and pulling her closer. The look in his eyes changed as they darkened with passion.

He was going to kiss her. The thought came in an urgent instant, fueling her own soaring needs.

She reached out and touched his arm, desperately trying to steady herself. But the second she did, his lips met hers. He threw her off balance once again by capturing her gasps and destroying her good intentions.

As she weakened and quit fighting, Sloan pulled back slightly and almost smiled. He seemed as surprised as she was by the exhilaration of their touching lips. Leaning in once again, he gently traced her lips with his tongue.

Excited, thrilled and totally lost, Lainie's lips parted as he slipped between them. When he deepened the kiss, sudden explosive heat enveloped her.

She shuddered and felt her bones, along with any common sense she should've had, melting under his passionate onslaught. Her body felt tender and achy.

When his hand moved to close over one breast, Lainie heard herself moan. Her nipples pressed hard against the thin cotton material of her bra as she arched under him.

Shaken and trembling, she laid her hand on his chest for support and let the pounding of his heart race through her fingers and up her arm. The beating rhythm pulsated, mingling with her own.

Everything about this seemed surreal. But Sloan was very real. And she'd never felt so alive.

He kissed his way across her chin and nibbled tiny caresses down her neck. She threw her head back and reveled in the exquisite sensations. Another moan escaped her lips as she murmured his name. "Sloan, oh…"

The sound of his own name brought him back to earth with a thump. "Easy, there." He heard himself slur the words and couldn't understand how he'd let himself get so carried away.

His whole body trembled along with hers, and both of them vibrated with needs he thought he'd long forgotten. She'd tasted like chocolate and coffee, and the feel of her under his hands had blown his mind to smithereens. He knew that if he didn't instantly pull back from this temptation, he would take her right here and right now.

"Easy," he mumbled again, as much as for himself as for her.

Sloan gently set her back in her seat and, with a supreme effort, levered himself back behind the wheel and clicked his seat belt closed again. They were sitting on the side of a public highway, for God's sake.

He *had* lost his mind. Taking a leave from the Rangers obviously meant he'd taken leave of his senses as well.

Closing his eyes for a second, he tried to shake off the last vestiges of a primitive heat that was so demanding and instinctual he couldn't imagine where it had come from. He'd spent much of his life burying all kinds of needs, so this savage wanting was a stunningly new experience. One he didn't care for at all.

"Uh…" he rasped in a shaky voice. He should say something, shouldn't he?

Hazarding a glance at the silent woman in the seat beside him, he wondered how to escape from such an embarrassing situation. She hadn't moved a muscle since he'd set her back in the seat. Unfortunately, he noticed that the front of her silk blouse was now wrinkled and the tails had been pulled from the waistband of her slacks.

This morning Sloan had been surprised when she'd changed into a fancy turquoise blouse and pantsuit at the police station. When he'd tried to explain they'd only be traveling for a few hours to the cabin and that maybe jeans would've been a better choice, she'd just shrugged.

It was an expensive outfit, he knew. And he hated to think he might've ruined it.

But as he watched her and looked for the right words to say, she sat with her back straight and her eyes focused forward out the front window. Tough little lady, he mused. All that flaming red hair and those sexy green eyes covered pure determination.

Another unwanted, sensual thrill rippled down to his loins. Fighting it and the images running through his head, Sloan leaned over and reached around to make sure her seat belt was secure.

He'd done it without thinking or giving her any warning. She reached for her own seat belt at that exact moment and was surprised by his sudden movement.

Lainie jerked, flailing her arms, and he tried to back out of the way. But it was too late. Her elbow swung wide and caught him on the chin.

"Ow..." he groaned as he ducked his head.

"Oh my God. I actually hit you. What did you think you were doing?"

"Checking your seat belt," he mumbled. "Protecting you."

"Look. I'm sorry my elbow connected with your chin, but I can protect myself, you know." She sat back and shook her head. "If you keep this up, you're going to drive me crazy."

Sloan wondered which of them would go over the edge first.

He sat there, fingering his sore jaw and considering an apology. But she straightened up and folded her arms over her chest.

"Are you going to get us something to eat or not?" she asked with a huff. The control and determination was back in her eyes.

Relieved that she didn't still have that fragile look, Sloan thought about being hungry, too. But it wasn't food he craved. He bit down on his tongue to keep his real urges quiet and cranked the wheel. Jamming the truck into gear, he stomped down on the gas.

Lord save him from all this togetherness.

Lainie was grateful for the crowded lunchroom. She was positive her face was still that flaming rose color it always got when she was embarrassed to death.

She took a bite of tuna salad sandwich and closed her eyes. Trying not to dwell on what a fool she'd made of herself wasn't working. Instead, her effort was focused on getting one thought out of her head:

she'd let him kiss her. Not only that, but she'd kissed him back—and enjoyed it. All he'd had to do was to stare at her with those dangerous brown eyes and she'd melted into his arms.

What an idiot she was. She berated herself for feeling the zip of electric current when he'd brushed that grinning, cocky mouth over hers. She'd wanted him badly. In fact, she couldn't remember ever wanting anyone quite that way before in her entire lifetime.

Her breasts still ached for the heat of his hand. Her lips still tingled from his kiss. Every muscle in her body that had felt lax and languid while he was near was now tensed and unfulfilled.

It must've been the shock of the past two days that had messed with her mind like this. Anyone would be entitled to go a little loopy after everything she'd been through. Right?

"You going to eat that sandwich or daydream over it?" Sloan asked.

The sound of his voice broke into her self-pity party. She ignored him and took another bite. They were out of town and safe now. Things were bound to get better.

He hadn't spoken more than two words since she'd hit him, back there in the truck. That was one more thing she should be embarrassed about.

She couldn't believe her rotten luck. She'd finally found someone who could glue her to the floor with just a kiss, and he was an uptight Texas Ranger who was impossible to read.

Never mind that her life had been in danger and she needed to check on Suzy. Love and lust and the man in the jeans and long-sleeved white shirt sitting next to her were all she could think about.

Swallowing another bite of sandwich, she picked up a couple of French fries and glared at him. "The food is fine here. Thank you for stopping." Lainie decided to be as polite and sweet as possible. Just to throw him off.

"Yeah? Well, eat up. We need to get going. It's dangerous to sit around anywhere for too long."

"Aren't you taking this bodyguard business a little bit too far? After all, who's going to find us way out here?"

Sloan unfolded his long legs from under the table and ignored her question. "I'll pay the tab." He stood and picked up the check. "Finish up."

He ambled up to the register, muttering under his breath as he went. He loved that sarcastic edge she had but couldn't imagine why he did. And he certainly wasn't about to let her know that.

Sloan threw down a few bills and waited for the bleached-blond cashier to make his change. He tried not to stare at the woman's chest, but her antacid-pink uniform gaped open where she'd left the top buttons undone.

Lainie sauntered up behind him. "I have to visit the ladies' room."

The cashier stopped cracking her gum long enough to point out the direction. And Sloan dropped the change back down on their table. Then he moved toward the front door, deciding to wait outside.

He situated himself with his back to the front door, trying to quell the outrageous thought that Lainie might try to escape out a window. He shrugged it off. She wasn't that stupid. Besides, he'd already checked out back earlier, while Lainie was getting settled at the table. He knew there were no exits and the windows were nailed shut.

After ten minutes of smoldering in the hot sun, he wondered if maybe he should try to find some way to get along with her. This idiotic situation they found themselves in was not really her fault.

He scratched the stubble on his jaw and rubbed across a surprising ache, reminding himself that some of the idiotic things were, in fact, her doing. Like not following his instructions to stay in her office in the first place.

Well, all that was past history. He'd made the decision to move on. Only this time, he would keep his temptations in check and his eye on what she was up to.

It was getting late and most of the lunch crowd had gone before Lainie finally joined him outside. "You ready to go now?" he grumbled.

She nodded and he took her elbow. As they moved onto the parking lot, Sloan noticed how empty the lot had suddenly become. His pickup stood alone beside the highway.

A trickle of sweat prickled as it rolled down the back of his neck. Things were just too quiet.

Picking up their pace as he took her by the hand, he chastised himself for not having parked around back. When they'd first pulled up an hour ago, he'd been grateful to find the first empty space to park. His brain must've been fried by that uncomfortable scene in the truck. And all he'd wanted right then was to get them both into a public place so he could regain some semblance of control.

"What's the big rush?" She leaned away from him as she kept up with his long strides.

"Get in the truck, Lainie." He practically ran the last twenty feet and gratefully shoved her into the front seat the minute they got there.

"What's wrong with you?" she inquired as he jumped in behind the wheel and locked the doors behind him.

Sloan turned the key in the ignition while he checked out their surroundings. "We have to be on our way." He slowly backed out of the spot and swung the front wheels in the direction of the highway.

Out of nowhere, the hollow ping of rifle shots pierced the quiet afternoon silence. Damn. Sons of bitches had spotted the truck. How lucky could they get?

Spinning the wheel in the opposite direction, he slammed down hard on the gas pedal. The truck roared across the gravel, shooting pebbles in every direction and heading right back the way they'd come.

He glanced over to check that Lainie was securely buckled in and found her oblivious to their peril. Sloan was relieved that she hadn't heard anything. He didn't want her to be afraid. He could handle this.

"What are you doing, Sloan?" she yelled over the squeal of tires. "You're going the wrong way. I've never been to Sequin, but this is the way we just came."

Ignoring her, he checked the rearview mirror, scanning for any sign of their assailants. But the road behind them was empty. When he stood on the gas pedal, the truck jumped and whined while he shifted into high gear. If his sudden change of direction had thrown them off, he wanted to make the most of it before they had a chance to recover.

"Slow down! You're going way over the speed limit. You'll get a ticket."

"I know what I'm doing and where I'm going," he snapped. "Don't you ever give up for one minute and let someone else handle things?"

She held on to the passenger door sway bar and wrinkled her nose. "Are you ever going to be anything but rude?"

After keeping his mouth firmly shut for the next ten minutes so he wouldn't say something he might regret, Sloan finally felt he could let off the gas. No one appeared to be following them.

Another quarter mile and he downshifted, pulling around a semitractor right into the Alternate 90 truckstop. They were safe, but in less than twenty minutes, all his good intentions about getting along with Lainie had blown the way of a West Texas wind.

He braked and slid neatly between two double trailers. Jamming on the parking brake, he drummed his fingers on the steering wheel and counted to ten.

"Why are we stopping here? Look, Sloan, if you're lost, I'd be happy to drive. Or maybe we could get a map from one of these truckers."

He glared at her, counted to ten once more and cleared his throat. "You want to know why I was speeding and why we had to backtrack in the wrong direction? All right, I'll tell you why. Because the whole point of us being together is to save your life.

"Not only do I know how to drive defensively, I

know how to evade attack. Someone was waiting to ambush us back there at the restaurant. They were firing at the truck as we pulled out of the lot. And I'd really prefer it if you didn't die while in my safekeeping. Got it?''

Her mouth had dropped open but she quickly shut it. ''You really have an overactive imagination, don't you? I didn't notice a thing out of the ordinary. No one could possibly follow us way out here. I think you're just trying to maintain some control. But I'm not afraid.''

Suddenly remembering the captain's words, Sloan kept his mouth shut. But his anger and adrenaline were still bubbling right below the surface.

He muttered a couple of swear words under his breath. He'd be damned if he would stoop to her level and tell her to just shut up for once and let the professional do his job. Instead, he shrugged a shoulder and shook his head.

''What'll we do now?'' She looked angry…and maybe a little lost again.

Sloan didn't want her to be either one. ''In a few minutes I'm going to call the captain and get him to send us another car.''

She tsked at him. ''Will he do such a silly thing?''

''Yeah, he will. And then we're going to travel to Sequin in the most roundabout way I can manage. I don't care if it takes us several days to get there instead of several hours. We're not taking any more chances.''

She nodded silently and shifted in her seat. Oh, man, would he ever love to know what was going on in that pretty head of hers. But he should've known it wouldn't take more than a couple of minutes for her to fill him in.

She swiveled in her seat to face him. "Sloan? Before lunch…uh…I mean…why'd you kiss me back there?"

Stuck, with no warning at all, Sloan was forced to tell her the truth. "Mostly it was to shut you up," he admitted. "But then it…became something else."

Slowly she touched her lips and nodded. "Yes. It did, didn't it?"

He let his hand wander over to her shoulder and gently squeezed. The urge was strong to kiss her again. But he wasn't a randy teenager and he'd promised himself there wouldn't be a next time. Above all else, he was determined to save her pretty neck.

He dragged his hand back to the wheel and shifted his gaze away from hers. "Look. I can't deal with this right now. I have to call the captain."

Sloan found himself fighting the contrary idea in the back of his mind that there definitely would be a next time for them. No matter what he'd vowed and no matter all his good intentions. The longer the two of them stayed together, the more certain he was that someday they'd be doing more than just kissing.

Every time he looked at her, his blood boiled and his body hardened. Imagining what it would feel like to lose himself in the satin of her skin and the thick lushness of her hair made even crazy ideas seem plausible.

He pulled his cell phone from his pocket and punched in the captain's number. "We'll talk about it later."

*   *   *

Lainie had given up trying to think well over an hour ago. Ever since they'd driven back to Sugarland and switched vehicles with Chet Johnson.

That is, if you could call this broken-down twelve-year-old SUV a vehicle. Sloan's call for a quick change of cars had apparently left his captain with few options. Chet had come to their rescue immediately. But the only thing he'd had available was his teenage son's secondhand SUV.

Where Sloan's pickup had ridden like a smooth luxury car, this rattletrap huffed and puffed and clanked along its merry way. Lainie wondered if her bones were strong enough to withstand the onslaught.

The air-conditioning didn't work. Rust had eaten through the front bumper. The muffler made the most horrific rumbling noise. As Lainie slid into the front passenger seat, she had to watch where she put her feet. The dangling wires and empty soda cans on the floor left little room for her to maneuver.

But Sloan never complained about any of it. He'd hefted her luggage out of his truck and into the SUV, then rolled down the windows and flipped on the CD player as they'd left the captain standing in a cloud of exhaust fumes. Trust a teenager not to give a flying fig about air-conditioning, but to have the biggest, state-of-the-art sound system that money could buy.

She suspected that Sloan cranked up the volume just to keep their conversation to a minimum. The tunes were all country music and not the rock she usually listened to. But she'd enjoyed them anyway.

As they traveled down the Texas back roads, she'd discovered that most of the melodies they were listening to weren't half-bad. The lyrics just begged listeners to sing along. She liked the ones about starting over after a failed marriage, finding new love, and that catchy tune about drinking long-neck beers in honky-tonk bars.

The questions starting piling up in her mind. "What exactly is a honky-tonk bar?" she asked after a minute.

"Excuse me?" Sloan had to turn down the music to hear.

"What goes on in honky-tonk bars?" When he looked at her as if she'd just arrived from the moon, she tried to explain. "You know. Like that guy was just singing about?"

He scowled. "Your father owns a bar, Lainie. I figured you'd know everything about them."

"No, I don't. When I was growing up, my dad was a line manager for an oil driller in Shreve-port…until he got laid off, that is. And I was always too busy to hang around in bars. I had to work my way through college, and after that I had to fight to get started in my career. Besides, I sort of thought drinking alcohol was a waste of money."

"So how'd your father end up owning a bar in Houston?"

"When I finally wangled my way into this job of writing an advice column for the paper, my whole family decided to pick up and move to Houston. I needed my family near me. My mom's old friend, your captain, lent my parents the money to buy a little business.

"I helped them choose the bar business idea," she admitted. "My father is so outgoing and personable, it seemed like a good fit at the time. But…''

She trailed off and shook her head sadly. So Captain Johnson was the private backer for Lainie's father? That explained a few things about their relationship.

"Owning your own business can be tricky," he told her.

Sighing deeply, Lainie sounded as if she was about to reveal something embarrassing. "Yeah. It's supposed to be a cozy neighborhood bar. But no matter how much redecorating they've done, the place always looks like a dump. And the worst thing is…''

Apparently at a loss for words, Sloan hated that she had that vulnerable look in her eyes again. It was even worse than that damned frightened animal stare she'd gotten when she'd realized someone wanted to kill her.

"Don't force yourself to tell me anything that's too hard to talk about." Sloan was already sorry he'd played that crazy song about honky-tonk bars.

"No." She shook her head. "It's good for people to talk about what's bothering them." She waved her hand in front of her face as if she were fanning herself. "I advise people in my column to be honest with themselves first, and then they can be honest with others."

He shrugged. "Whatever." He'd always figured too much honesty could mean talking about things that were better left unsaid and buried.

"My father is an alcoholic," she said flatly. "Oh, he has never admitted it to himself. But we all know it. I'm sure that's what caused him to have the stroke at such a young age. Too much booze."

"Uh…I wouldn't think owning a bar would be a real good occupation for someone addicted to alcohol."

She rolled her eyes and grimaced. "Exactly. Unfortunately, none of us realized what a problem he had until he'd been running the bar for quite a while."

Heaving another long-suffering sigh, she shrugged. "All that doesn't matter now." With a quick look out the window, she swung back around to him. "What about the honky-tonks? Have you ever actually been to one?"

"I've been to a few places that might qualify."

"What're they like?"

"They're not particularly interesting. Some are pretty rough places. Most are just cheap, noisy dives. Working men—like cowboys, truckers and oil riggers—go there looking to spend their free time by hard drinking and hard playing." Sloan studied her a minute. "I don't think you'd care for it."

And he didn't care much for all this talking. It was too intimate. Too close. If he didn't watch himself, he'd be spilling his guts about his own sad background.

"Just don't take the music so literally," he muttered as he cranked the volume up again.

As Sloan drove, he hummed along to the loud music and effectively shut out any more questions. Lainie began to wonder if there weren't a lot of things she'd missed out on by working all the time. Not just cheap bars, but life.

It was ironic that a woman like her, who was famous for giving advice on many subjects, hadn't even experienced some of the problems she was asked to solve. Although…she did have a psychology degree, and she knew how and whom to ask for expert help. And she'd be the first to admit that she knew the value of working hard and being loyal to family. But when it came to her own personal relationships and knowing how to have fun, she'd just discovered that she was a novice.

She chanced a peek over at Sloan, who was wearing dark glasses to block the glare as he drove into the setting sun. Maybe this trip would be her opportunity to learn about life firsthand. Then it wouldn't be the useless waste of time she'd imagined.

Studying his strong chin and deep-set eyes, Lainie wondered whether Sloan would turn out to be a chance at a real-life relationship…or if he would be her absolute worst nightmare.

Five

With the warm, spring air blowing through her hair and the waning sunshine beating down on her right arm, Lainie tried to enjoy the ride and not think too much about the man sitting beside her. But she was curious about him.

Why hadn't some smart Texas girl snagged such a great catch? Sloan was certainly good-looking, in a rugged sort of way. As a matter of fact, judging by that intoxicating kiss they'd shared, he'd be classified as downright hot.

Disgusted with herself for not being able to think of anything but Sloan, she tried to focus on the scenery instead. There wasn't much to see, though. They were traveling down a two-lane country road, through fields plowed to bare dirt and ready to be planted.

Occasionally she'd see an oil well or two off in

the distance. Some of the pumps they passed were bobbing up and down, dredging up black crude from deep below the surface. Still other pumps she saw sat unmoving and forlorn, like a child's wind-up toy that had just run down.

But the sun still shone on this late afternoon and the music was pleasant. So Lainie kept watching out the window and tried to busy herself by picking out shapes in the clouds and trying to figure out which directions they were heading by following the sun.

Another hour went by, along with several small towns with strange names. Like the crossroads town that didn't have so much as one tree but was called Shady Point. And Dry Gap was sure a funny name for a tiny village on the banks of the very wet Brazos River. And they'd stopped for bottled water at a convenience store in a town called Bay City that was miles and miles away from any bay.

As the hours and miles rolled by, Lainie began to spot a profusion of color growing right alongside the roadway. Wildflowers sprouted from little nooks and crannies. After they'd topped a small crest, flowers were suddenly everywhere she looked.

"How beautiful!" she exclaimed cheerfully.

"What?" Sloan lowered the music once again.

"Oh, please stop here. I've never seen anything like this before."

"What are you talking about? There's nothing here but old cow pastures and a smattering of oil wells."

"The flowers. They're wonderful. Just look at them. Oranges, yellows, and see those bluish-purple ones? Aren't they something?"

Sloan found a dirt road where he could pull off

to the side. Lainie was out and walking back toward the full bed of color before he had a chance to turn off the engine.

"Hold on a second." He fumbled for the keys and swung out of the truck. "Lainie, wait up." She wasn't paying a bit of attention to the other cars on the road or to where she was walking.

"You act like you've never seen flowers growing by a roadside before," he admonished when he caught up.

Spinning around twice and throwing her hands above her head, she plopped right down in the dirt. "I haven't," she said and bent to smell the Indian paintbrush. "At least not like these."

"I don't believe that wildflowers have a particular scent," he advised. "The Texas countryside is full of flowers like these in the spring. Lady Bird Johnson made beautifying the roadside landscapes her pet project some thirty years ago. Now you can find them just about everywhere in Texas if you simply take the time to look."

He stared down at her. "They're really nothing special." When she frowned sadly, he decided to temper that statement. "But I do have to agree about the bluebonnets being especially pretty this year."

"Bluebonnets. Is that what these are? How fantastic."

"Come on, now. That's enough." They'd been stopped for too long and he was starting to worry. "We can't be caught lingering by the side of the road. You never know who might see us."

"I just need a few minutes, Sloan. It's so peaceful here. So special. Why don't you join me?" She laughed out loud and leaned back on her elbows.

Her whole body disappeared into the blanket of flowers.

It was the first time Sloan had heard her really laugh. What a beautiful sound she made. He figured her musical laughter was better than any old country-western song could ever have been.

The more she giggled, the more outlandish and free spirited she seemed. And she looked younger than before, too. He would've called her carefree and untroubled if he hadn't been so aware that some evil chased her.

Her laughter made him smile. And not much in this world could claim to do that.

Sloan suddenly wondered what he would have to do in order to keep that laughter on her lips. And why he hadn't heard her do it before now. He almost gave in to his immediate need—that most urgent desire to drop down beside her and concentrate on giving her pleasure by stroking, touching and kissing that fabulously soft skin. She would smile just for him then. He was sure of it.

But the nagging reminder of why they were together had him shaking his head and extending his hand toward her instead. "It's almost dark, Lainie. We have to be going. Besides, you're ruining that expensive outfit you have on."

She quit smiling and grimaced. Taking his hand, she let him pull her up and out of the flower bed.

Once she was back on her feet, she tried to dust off her slacks but the fine material was stained with grass and pollen. "Darn. I was so thrilled by the flowers I never gave a thought to this suit."

"Uh, maybe you should stick to wearing more casual clothes until we can get you back to your normal routine. We're headed for a cabin that's probably pretty rustic compared to what you're used to. I wouldn't want you to destroy all your good clothes.''

"But linen and silk pantsuits *are* my casual clothes.'' She shrugged out of her jacket and inspected the back. "Well, except for my gym clothes. And Mom didn't pack those. I'm sure she wouldn't have thought I'd be rolling around in the dirt.''

Sloan couldn't quite understand what she was trying to tell him. "What about your jeans?'' He figured they must be having a communication problem. "Surely your mother packed at least one pair of jeans for you to wear.''

Lainie cocked her head and squinted up into the last rays of sun behind him. "I only own one pair of denim pants. They belong to a Western suit I bought to wear to a barbecue my boss was throwing. But they're covered with sparkles and have sequins on the back pockets. They're not what I'd call casual.''

He was incredulous. "You don't own any work jeans? Good Lord, Lainie, you live in Texas. How do you get by?''

"People recognize me wherever I go. I have to maintain a professional image. I'm a newspaper columnist, not a rancher.''

He followed her to the SUV, making sure she got safely inside. When he'd buckled himself back into the driver's seat, he turned to her. "There's a discount store in a town down the road. We'll go on a shopping trip after we get settled into a motel for the night. You need some decent jeans. If you're going to blend in with Texans, you'd better dress like one.''

They pulled into the parking lot of the Quiet Rest Motel in Edna, and Sloan turned off the engine. He unpinned his badge and slipped it into his pocket, surprising Lainie. She'd guessed that the man probably wore his badge everywhere.

''Are you going undercover?'' she teased.

He turned his head and glared at her with those dark and serious eyes. ''If we're being tracked, they'll be looking for a Ranger and a city woman.'' He reached behind the seat for his white Stetson.

''Don't you think the long-sleeved white shirt and the white hat might be dead giveaways?''

He hesitated, then dropped the hat back on the seat and flipped his denim jacket off its hook. ''No sense taking chances. Sit tight. I'll be right back.''

While Sloan checked them into the motel, Lainie gazed at her surroundings. They'd come into Edna, Texas, via a small back road. But the town, which, according to a sign, boasted a population of six thousand was cut in two by a wide four-lane highway. Judging by the billboards and the bait-and-tackle stores, Edna catered exclusively to tourists who were there to visit nearby Lake Texana.

At least the Quiet Rest Motel was a little more modern than the disaster where they'd spent last night in Houston. Was that only twenty-four hours ago? It seemed as if she'd been on the run with Sloan for days.

Sloan came back to the car with a scowl on his face, jumped into the driver's seat and slammed the door behind him. ''Hell.''

Lainie saw a key card in his hand and knew he'd gotten a room. But before she had time to ask what the problem was, Sloan told her.

"I intended to get us two connecting rooms," he said through gritted teeth. "The town's having some kind of bird-watching adventure festival this week. The only two empty rooms they had left were on separate floors."

He held out the one keycard. "I guess we're bunking together again."

"We could've stayed in the separate rooms." She spoke quietly as she took the card. "Or we could've gone on to the next town."

He glared at her. "If we'd gotten the separate rooms, I wouldn't have been able to sleep, wondering if you were all right. And the nearest town with a motel is Victoria. They don't have any vacancies there, either, what with the Texas state high school softball championship."

Lainie laid a hand on his arm. "It'll be okay, Sloan. We managed last night. We'll get by for one more night."

His look was unreadable and he didn't utter another word. Easing his arm out from under her hand, he cranked the ignition and the SUV roared to life. They pulled up in front of a room at the end of a long outside hallway. Together they lugged her suitcases into the air-conditioned room. It amused her when she saw that the room had two double beds. Spending the night together was going to be a piece of cake this time.

"You want to rest, take a shower or eat first?" Sloan asked.

"None of the above," she said with a grin. "I want to shop."

Both of Sloan's eyebrows shot up. "Aren't you tired?"

"I'm getting a second wind. Let's go." When he scowled, she narrowed her eyes in determination. "You promised."

The discount store was about a mile out of town on the four-lane highway. It was as big as two football fields, and Lainie guessed that every person in Texas who wasn't bird-watching or at the softball championships had decided to shop there tonight.

Still, she had great fun elbowing her way to the heavily laden shelves full of women's jeans. Shopping in Houston at the tasteful boutiques and upscale department stores had never been much fun. But this was a challenge.

Sloan stood back out of the way with his arms folded over his chest and a blank expression on his face. She wasn't sure if it was that he didn't approve of her shopping methods or if he was trying not to laugh at her incompetence.

Just when Lainie located a pair of jeans in her size, a big woman in bib overalls grabbed them and added the pair to a huge stack she was carrying under one arm.

"Drop those pants," Lainie ordered. "They're mine. I saw them first."

The woman ignored her and grabbed three more pairs of stone-washed jeans in varying sizes. Lainie wondered whether she could get the pushy woman to let go of the bundle by jamming one of her stack heels down on her arch.

No, that would be rude…and it might be dangerous. Plus, the woman had on heavy cowboy boots and probably wouldn't feel a thing.

Lainie took a time out and stood back a few feet to survey the situation. Over her shoulder, she saw Sloan with a twinkling glint in his eyes. Damned man *was* laughing at her.

A vision of the smile he'd given her, right before he frazzled her brain with that mind-melting kiss, slid into her conscious mind. Her body was still smoking from that scorcher nearly six hours later. Lainie tried to think of any other man in her life whose kiss had affected her that way.

She'd had her share of boyfriends and passionate kisses. But hours afterward, the best she would've said about any of them was that they were very *nice*. Perhaps even pleasant.

None of those adjectives came close to describing Sloan's kiss.

Just then, a tall thin woman dressed in black stretch jeans and a fuzzy red sweater came up beside her. "The place is a real madhouse tonight. Ain't it, sugar?"

Lainie threw her hands on her hips. "I just haven't figured out how to beat the crowd at its own game yet. I wish my sister was here. She's the shopper in the family. I'm lost without her."

The big-haired brunette scrutinized Lainie's figure. "You look about the same size as my daughter. Size eight?"

"Yeah." On a good day.

"Well there's a stack of sixes and eights over on that table in the middle of the aisle. I don't guess the more 'mature size' ladies have discovered them yet."

"Thanks." Lainie nearly ran to the table and picked up three pairs before anyone else found them. Then she rounded up a few long-sleeved knit shirts and a couple of short-sleeved T-shirts in various pastel colors.

"Mighty quick shopping trip," Sloan murmured when she told him she was done.

On their way to the cashier, he picked up three men's T-shirts from a sale rack they'd passed. When she asked him if he needed more time to shop, he just shook his head. "Nope. There's nothing to this shopping stuff," he said with a chuckle.

It had been an amazingly fast shopping trip, she thought, considering the crowds. But when they arrived at the cashier stands in the front of the store, all their speed came to a grinding halt. The lines wound around and intertwined back on themselves. It looked as if they were in for a long wait.

Twenty minutes later Lainie's feet hurt, and she was about to faint from lack of food. Fortunately, only a few people were left in line in front of them.

She turned around to see how many people were still waiting in their line and spotted the same helpful brunette right behind them. They greeted each other like old friends and the woman introduced herself as Rhonda Marie Swisher.

Sloan inched forward and shot Lainie a dark look when she introduced herself by her first name. What did he take her for? She knew better than to say her last name.

The two battle-weary shopping pals struck up a bored conversation about jeans and how appropriate they were to wear in different situations. In a deep East Texas drawl, Lainie's new friend claimed she couldn't imagine anyplace in the whole state where jeans wouldn't fit in.

All their discussion about dancing and Texas-style restaurants caused Lainie to remember something she wanted to ask. "You live around here, Rhonda?"

"All my life, sugar."

"Well, are there any places nearby that would qualify as a honky-tonk in your opinion? And would jeans be the appropriate dress for a place like that?"

Rhonda's eyes widened before she threw a quick glance in Sloan's direction. "There's a couple of places around that might be considered honky-tonks. But I don't know if you really…"

"Have you ever been to any of them?" Lainie cut in.

"Well…yeah. I might've been to a place called Six-Shooter Junction. Weeknights they serve a special drink every hour and the first one you order is free. They've got the best draft beer and tequila in two counties. And there's karaoke two nights a week, too. But not tonight. Tonight is ladies' choice."

"Sounds like fun. And you think my new jeans would be okay to wear there?"

Rhonda agreed that jeans would be perfect and gave Lainie directions on how to get to the place. Their conversation was cut short when they finally arrived at the cashier.

Sloan pulled Lainie closer in line. "Put your stuff on the counter," he growled. "I'll get it, but you can pay me back later."

"Doesn't Six-Shooter Junction sound like fun?" she asked him breezily.

"Lainie, there is absolutely no way we're going to some grimy roadhouse bar tonight. Just get that silly notion right out of your head."

He was still grumbling as he opened the heavy wooden door and let Lainie go ahead of him into the darkened interior of Six-Shooter Junction.

The woman was like a pit bull when she got her teeth into something. There had been no stopping her from finding a way to get to this roadhouse tonight. So, rather than have her take a cab or hitch a ride, he'd reluctantly agreed to bring her.

And in order to speed up the process, he'd stood guard outside the SUV while she'd changed her clothes in the back seat. He had to admit she looked pretty sweet in those new hip-hugging jeans. The curves he'd wondered about when she'd had on that pair of slacks and loose jacket were now plainly visible. The dark-blue denim strained over her rounded bottom. Sloan had to stop himself from ogling.

She'd slipped on a new kelly green, long-sleeved shirt that brought out the color in her eyes. It was made from some stretchy material that strained over her firm breasts. A vee in the neckline slit down to the rise right above her bra, drawing his gaze. But he managed to look over her left shoulder and into the bar a split second before she caught him staring.

It had already been a long day of driving and trying to ignore the heat she'd exuded sitting next to him. Now, how the hell was he supposed to last through a long night with her?

After the first blast of air-conditioning hit them and Sloan's eyes had adjusted to the low lighting, he guided her through the smoke-filled bar with loud music coming from ceiling-mounted speakers six-feet tall. The songs were old country. The newest song Sloan recognized was a Travis Tritt recording that had been popular several years ago.

"It's so dark in here." Lainie fiercely held on to his arm and stumbled over the splintered wooden floorboards only one time. "Can you see an empty table?"

"Keep moving. We're headed for the restaurant side. I think we need some food."

"Oh, good. I'm famished."

A young blond woman, dressed in skintight jeans and a fringed halter top, met them at the edge of a room filled with booths. It was slightly better lit than the bar had been. "Dinner for two?"

"Can we order drinks in here, too?" Lainie asked.

The hostess carried an armful of menus. She looked at Lainie as if she'd just asked if they served human sacrifice for lunch. "You're kidding," she said as she swiveled on her toes and looked out over the packed booths. "Follow me."

Sloan kept one hand on Lainie's shoulder as they picked their way through the narrow aisles of the restaurant, trying to follow the hostess who took off at a dead run. The sound of his boots clacking on the wood floor and the din of people talking over their dinners competed with the music as Sloan's head started to pound. Too crowded to be comfortable, he thought.

He'd been in lots of joints that were built on the same theme, all over the state. This one didn't seem special, but Lainie was gawking around as if she'd never seen anything like it before.

They scooted into a tiny booth in the back, and his nose was assaulted by the tangy smell of barbecue mingling with the heavy smell of greasy fried potatoes. The hostess placed two plastic-covered menus down in front of them. "What can I get you from the bar?"

"I want to try one of your tequilas," Lainie yelled over the noise.

The hostess lowered her chin and frowned down at her. Then she turned to Sloan for a translation. "Tequila what?" she asked with a wink.

The waitress's questions weren't what concerned him at the moment. "Lainie, don't you think you should start off a little slower? You need something in your stomach first. Why don't you just order whatever they have on tap?"

"No." She glared up at the waitress, who suddenly seemed terribly bored. "I want to try the tequila. Just bring me a bottle of the best brand you carry."

The hostess shrugged, and when she did, Sloan noted the tattoo of a hummingbird on the swell of her left breast. "And what'll you have, honey?" She smiled at him and batted her lashes.

Oh, brother. He knew damned well what she was offering. But as a Ranger he wasn't accustomed to getting hit on. It was a sharp reminder that he'd removed the badge.

He gave the woman a slight shake of the head as an answer to her unspoken question, and glanced at Lainie out of the corner of his eye. As if he didn't already have his hands full with her.

"I'm the designated driver," he snorted. "Just bring me a tonic water." As the hostess nodded and turned, he grabbed her wrist. "Make that a *pint* of tequila, and be sure the seal is tight."

The hostess left to get their drinks, and a skinny teenage boy appeared to take their food order. The kid was so busy staring down at Lainie that he forgot what the specials were tonight. After ten minutes the teenager's tongue was dragging on his notepad, and Sloan was afraid they would never get to eat.

After a lot of discussion and indecision, Sloan finally took charge and told the kid to bring them two brisket plates. Lainie looked a little put out that he'd rushed her but, damn it, he was hungry.

Before Sloan could try to stretch his legs under this tiny table, the hostess reappeared with their drinks. She plopped down a bottle of gold-label Blue Agave, a glass filled with ice and a plate with sliced Mexican lemons and a mound of salt.

Then she set his tonic water on a napkin. "Holler if you want a refill, honey. My name's Holly," the hostess told him and then disappeared.

Lainie picked up the pint bottle and began to pour the tequila over ice. "What're the lemons and salt for?"

"That's the way you drink tequila. First a sip—straight out of the bottle—then quickly suck on the lemon and salt to ease it down."

"Really? How cool." She tipped the bottle and took a big gulp.

"Uh, don't you think you ought to pace yourself with that? Didn't you tell me that you never drink?"

Her eyes grew round with shock, and the expression on her face was priceless. She grabbed a lemon slice, swished it quickly in the salt and stuck it into her mouth whole.

A few seconds later her eyes were watering, but she had a grin as wide as a six-lane highway on her face. ''That was great,'' she rasped. ''This is going to be a fun night.''

Six

Lainie stuffed the last bite of onion loaf into her mouth and sighed with pleasure. Everything had been perfect so far at Six-Shooter Junction.

Everything but the company. Sloan hadn't said two words since the food arrived. He'd screwed up his mouth with every sip of tequila she'd taken. And he scowled each time the waiter made a trip to their table.

She'd hoped that he would loosen up a little with the good music and food. But he just seemed to get more and more tense as the time went by.

Her decision this afternoon to have some fun while on this so-called vacation was apparently causing him some discomfort. He was so uptight about being her guard that he couldn't relax. But there didn't seem to be much danger here.

Now that she was sure her sister and everyone

back at the office were okay, and it had been miles
and miles since they'd had any run-ins with the bad
guys, why shouldn't she sample all the fun things
she'd been missing out on for most of her life? She
hadn't planned this little sabbatical. It had been
rammed down her throat. But why was it so wrong
to make the most of it?

Sloan set down his fork and glared at her. "You
about ready to leave?"

"Leave? Certainly not. It's early yet."

"Look, Lainie. The longer we stay in a public
place, the easier we make it for whoever's stalking
you to find us. We need to keep away from crowds
and stay out of sight."

He was back to being in control.

"Okay…I guess you're right. But I need to excuse myself before we go. You don't have to guard
me in there, too, do you?"

He narrowed his eyes. "Don't be cute. I'll take
care of the bill and meet you by the front door."

She inched through the crowd to the bar and
asked the bartender to show her the way to the rest
room. Feeling a little dizzy and shaky on her feet,
she chalked it up to sitting for too long today. Tomorrow she'd have to insist they stop and get some
exercise.

Sloan checked his watch for the third time and
stood aside while a burly guy with tattoos of snakes
on both arms jostled him as he came through the
front door. Lainie had staggered away from the table
twenty minutes ago, and he couldn't help being concerned.

For a woman who never drank, she could've easily put a two-hundred-pound roustabout under the table tonight. She'd damned near finished off an entire pint of tequila.

He smiled to himself when he thought about watching her hips sway as she'd made her way through the crowd. But in short order, the smile had turned to a frown as he remembered that most of the male heads in the bar had also turned to check her out.

Oh, man. What the hell did he care whether every guy on earth stared at her? It wasn't as if they were on a date.

He couldn't remember the last time he'd been on a date, if the truth were known. But he did remember thinking of it as an ego builder if other guys checked out his companion.

Why was it so different with Lainie? As he glanced at his watch one last time, Sloan came to the conclusion that it must be his bodyguarding duties making what he felt about her seem so unusual. That must be it.

He headed off in the direction of the ladies' room, half expecting to find her passed out on the floor. But when he spotted her on the dance floor, he felt the tension leave his shoulders. She was surrounded by a group of people who were attempting to learn a line dance.

While he stood off to the side and enjoyed the sight of her laughing with everyone else, some skinny dude walked over and handed her a long-neck beer. Lainie shyly smiled up at the guy and took a swig. What the hell?

Sloan stopped waiting and cleared the distance between them in two strides. "It's time to go," he growled when he moved beside her and slid his arm around her waist.

She stiffened under his hand, but didn't say a word.

"Hey, man, what's going on?" the skinny guy with the beer whined. "I saw her first."

"See someone else," Sloan grumbled.

The other man turned to Lainie for one last try. She smiled tightly, shook her head, and handed him back the beer she'd been holding.

"Sorry, buddy." The guy nodded to Sloan. "Didn't know things were like that." He moved past them both and disappeared into the crowd.

"Let's go." Sloan tightened his grip on her and took a step toward the front door.

"There's absolutely nothing wrong with me learning a new dance. I want to stay awhile." She tried unsuccessfully to slip out of his grasp.

He stopped dragging her for the moment because he didn't want to cause a scene. "You've had too much to drink," he snapped. "Before you left the table you agreed that it was time to leave. Remember?"

"I changed my mind. Now I want to dance." She looked up at him with heavily lidded eyes and tried to focus on his face. "Am I your prisoner again?"

She leaned back away from him, swaying slightly. Putting her wrists together, she held them out in front of her chest. "You want to cuff me, Ranger Abbott?"

He couldn't tell her that the idea held a lot of promise and would definitely be in his fantasies from now on. But he did have to find a way of keeping her quiet and getting her the hell out of this joint without making a fuss.

Lainie suddenly looked a little dazed. He clamped his hands on her shoulders and dragged her to his chest. ''All right. Fine. One dance and we're out of here. Okay?''

She melted into him and laid her head on his shoulder. ''Okay,'' she sighed.

Sloan held her tightly at the waist as she reached up and hooked both her arms around his neck. He felt her nipples harden when her breasts mashed against his chest. And, at about the same time, the sweat broke out on his forehead. It was mighty close in here, wasn't it?

Fortunately, the music shifted to something slow, and he leaned in close enough to breathe the perfume of her soft hair. She smelled so good, so much like the scent of hay and fresh air, that he suddenly felt a little light-headed himself.

Sloan did his best to concentrate on where they were and the nature of his mission. They were in a public place. She was being stalked. He was her bodyguard, and the only thing standing between her and possible injury.

But his thoughts weren't helping. When the idea of her being injured or killed filled his consciousness, he tightened his hold.

She moaned and snuggled in closer. Her warm breath tickled his neck and ran chills down his spine. He was aroused beyond belief. He bent to place a gentle kiss against her hair.

The music suddenly changed tempo and someone accidentally knocked into them on the dance floor.

The couple excused themselves and moved off, doing a quick version of a Texas two-step.

The mood was broken. He glanced down at Lainie and realized she was just about to collapse.

"That's it. We're leaving," he barked. Grabbing her before she had a chance to complain or to pass out, Sloan practically carried her to the parking lot.

While thanking God for the spring chill in the night air, he buckled her into the SUV. Then Sloan jumped behind the wheel and roared out of the lot. With one quick glance to check on her sleeping form, he sped down the highway, swearing to do a better job of keeping his hands to himself.

He needed to have more control than this. Dammit. No woman was going to turn him into an idiot. Especially not this danged fool redhead.

When they arrived at the motel, Sloan tried to get her out of the SUV with a minimum of fuss. The parking lot was quiet and he hoped to make it into their room with no one noticing.

"Lainie, can you walk?" he whispered.

"Certainly," she declared in a hoarse voice. "I'm perfectly fine. Just a little tired is all."

She slid out of the seat, and her legs buckled under her. If he hadn't reached for her at just that moment, she would've landed in a heap on the pavement.

"Yeah. You're fine." He picked her up in his arms. "We'll be inside in a second."

She leaned into his chest as he locked and slammed the door behind them. Her breath tickled his neck, putting him on edge again. Well, at least she was being quiet. Maybe they could still make it to the room without being spotted.

When they reached the motel room, Sloan had to shift her in his arms in order to dig into his jeans pocket for the key card. Getting through the door one-handed would be a little tricky.

He balanced her against the wall and jammed the card into the slot. Lainie lifted her head to look at him.

"You are a beautiful man. You know that?"

"Uh-huh." He managed to get the door open.

"Someone needs to dedicate a song to you, Sloan." She rolled in his arms as he tried to get them both through the threshold. "This kiss. This kiss," she warbled at the top of her lungs.

"Shush," he muttered. "I don't think Faith Hill would appreciate you murdering her song that way."

He stepped through the doorway and managed to get her in position over the bed before she wiggled out of his arms. She plopped down and immediately sat up.

"Oh, I'm dizzy." She looked up at him. "But not too dizzy to know that I want to kiss you again."

Sloan locked and chained the door. "How's your stomach?"

"My stomach? It's perfect, thank you. Why?"

She reached out for him and he backed away. "I have a feeling you may not make it through the night without being sick."

"No way." She stood and took a shaky step. "My stomach is made of iron."

The minute those words were out of her mouth, she sucked in a gasping breath and pushed her flattened palm into her stomach. Her face turned a deathly white. Sloan watched as her eyes widened and she clamped the other hand over her mouth.

"That's exactly what I was talking about. Let's go." He rushed her into the bathroom, flipped up the toilet seat and bent her over the bowl.

She held herself up on one elbow. He turned to soak a washcloth in cold water, then held it against her forehead.

"Oh God. Go away," she moaned as she took the cloth from his hand.

"You okay?"

"No. But I will be," she said weakly. "Just leave me alone. Please?"

"I'll be right outside the door if you need me." He shut the door behind him and went over to her bags, still on the floor waiting to be unpacked.

He put her overnight case on the bed and stared down at it. Wanting to get her something more comfortable to wear but not wanting to violate her personal things, he hesitated. The sound of the toilet flushing wiped all the indecision right out of him.

Sloan opened the case and tried to be as neat as possible about unpacking. When he got to her lingerie, though, his heart started racing at the sight of wispy scraps of silk.

Uh-oh. Didn't the woman own a decent robe?

He gently fingered past a stack of white lace underpants, trying not to think of how she would look in them. He tried to ignore the racy black bra and nearly choked when he came to a bright-red lace contraption that would cover her from the breasts to the crotch…just barely.

A man would have to be dead not to be stirred

by the image of Lainie in that thing, lying below him and waiting for him to take it off her. Sloan whistled through his teeth and blew out a deep breath. He was making himself crazy and it wouldn't do.

He grabbed something made from a flimsy lavender material that looked as though it might qualify as a nightgown. Then he knocked on the bathroom door.

"Can I come in?" He didn't get an answer so he opened it and peeked inside.

She was sitting with her back propped against the wall and her eyes closed.

"Lainie?"

She groaned but didn't answer him.

"Okay, sweetheart." He set the nightgown down on the sink and reached for her. "Up you go. Looks like we're going to have to take drastic measures with you."

"Huh?" she mumbled.

The first thing he did was pull off her shoes. Then he sat her up and dragged the T-shirt over her head. The sight of her breasts, peeking through the white lacy bra she wore, gave him a moment's pause. But he shut the images out of his mind and set about being as detached as humanly possible.

"Well. That's going to have to do," he said as he hauled her to her feet. "I sure hope your new jeans don't shrink."

He lifted her feetfirst into the tub and held her with one hand as he turned the faucet, adjusting until it was lukewarm. "Easy now." He watched her face as he turned on the shower.

Her eyes popped open and she shrieked. "What

the—? Stop that.'' She slapped at his hands. ''That's enough. Let me out of here.''

''This is good for you.''

She was slippery now and tried to get out of his grip. He kicked off his boots and stepped into the shower. Moving close behind her body, he put his arms around her waist and held on tightly as the shower spray pelted down on them.

Lainie quit wiggling after a moment and leaned back against his chest, letting the water slide over her. Oh, man, had *this* been a mistake.

The water sent prickles of sensation to his groin as his clothes grew wet and clung to him. The feel of the soft skin on her bare stomach caused sweat to roll down the back of his neck, even under the cool water.

Finally, he couldn't stand the pain of being this close, yet not really close at all. So he dragged her bottom hard against his groin. She tensed when she felt his arousal, and he realized she was holding her breath.

The knowledge that she was shocked into breathlessness stopped him more effectively than anything else. ''Lainie, can you stand by yourself?''

She sucked in some air. ''Yes,'' she said tentatively.

''Good. I'm out of here. When you feel better, get out and dry yourself off. I'll be outside.'' He let her go and managed to step out of the tub. ''Uh... I won't be far. Call if you need me.''

He grabbed up his boots as he stormed out of the bathroom. Standing in the bedroom, soaking wet and breathing hard, he tried to clear his head.

Doing his best not to think of how close he'd just

come to ripping both their clothes off and taking advantage of her weakened state, he quickly changed into dry clothes. Being this close to Lainie was making him forget everything. All his own problems. All that he owed to Captain Johnson and to the memory of his mother. Everything.

What was he going to do about it?

After taking the two aspirin tablets that Sloan provided, along with a cup of hot, black coffee, Lainie crawled into bed, exceedingly grateful that the room had stopped spinning. Sloan had been so solicitous and tender with her that it almost made her cry. Even in her present unclear state, she knew she would remember this night and his kind attentions for the rest of her life.

One other thing was clear. She would never, *ever* drink tequila again. In fact, she figured that the next time she let alcohol pass her lips would be in celebration of her sixty-fifth birthday party.

Sloan made sure she was tucked in before he turned out the lights. With the motel room's black-out curtains drawn, it was too dark to be sure, but she thought she heard him crawl into the other bed.

''Good night, Lainie. Sleep tight.''

She wanted to say something. To thank him for being so kind during one of her worst moments. But she was exhausted and so sleepy that she couldn't quite manage to open her mouth before everything faded into black oblivion.

Lainie woke sometime later and rolled on her side to look at the lit-up clock. She tried to focus on the hands, but the pain right behind her eyes was ferocious. At least her stomach wasn't rolling, she gratefully acknowledged.

Squeezing her eyes shut, she tried to drift back into nothingness. But dark, watery images invaded her mind.

First came the hummingbird. Scary and larger than life, it flew at her face. Her first impulse was anger, not fear, as she batted it away, but that seemed silly. Why should she be mad at a harmless hummingbird?

Next, big blue eyes, eyes so like her own green ones and yet not, floated into view. They were filled with sorrow and pain. Tears and heartache were clearly written there.

Suzy? Trying to focus, Lainie felt sure the eyes belonged to her sister. But why? She knew Suzy was not hurt badly and should be out of the hospital by now. So why did she seem to be in pain?

As if in answer to her question, Lainie's vision cleared and she saw Suzy, alone and crying as if her heart was broken beyond repair. Lainie reached out but couldn't touch her.

Even in her dreams she was positive her sister should be fine. Wasn't she? Suzy was supposed to have all the family around her. Their parents. Her husband, Jeff. Where was everyone?

Something seemed very wrong.

Lainie hadn't had the time to really talk to her sister about her life in quite a while. There was always so much to do. And Suzy always appeared to be so happy. She never said too much, but Lainie was positive Suzy's life was going well. She was the one steady person that Lainie hadn't needed to worry about.

However, this vision of her sister made it appear that Suzy was miserable and alone. And what's more, it felt as if she'd been that way for a long time.

The image melted away and Lainie tried to recapture it. She badly wanted to find out what was wrong and to fix it. That's what she did the best, after all.

But the dream was over, leaving Lainie shaky, frustrated and wide awake. She sat up on the side of the bed and could finally read the clock. Five-thirty. For a second she panicked, wondering if that meant in the afternoon. But as her eyes adjusted to the dark, she saw the lone figure in the other double bed.

Sloan—asleep. It must be early in the morning.

She dragged the blanket up and over her for warmth and stood on wobbly feet. Needing to talk to him, to hear his calm voice telling her everything was all right, Lainie inched her way over to his bed and knelt down beside it.

Now that she'd come this close, she was about to lose her nerve. She didn't know the correct etiquette for waking a man up out of a sound sleep. Especially this man.

She reached out tentatively in the dark and shook the lump in the bed. "Sloan," she whispered.

Instantly he sat up and turned on the bedside light. "What? What's wrong?" He reached under the pillow and drew his gun. "Did you hear something?"

"No. Nothing's wrong," she quickly told him. "I just needed to talk to someone."

This wasn't what she'd expected or wanted. But as she sat back on her heels and watched him look around the room, then slide his gun away, Lainie decided that the view might be worth all this trouble. The sheet had slipped down and pooled around his waist, leaving his bare chest uncovered.

The muscles in his upper body rippled under the protection of curly dark-brown hair. Whew. She hadn't realized exactly how built Sloan truly was.

Before that thought could settle into her belly, she remembered the feel of his body against her back last night in the shower. She didn't remember a whole lot from last night, but the sensual and erotic memory of his hard muscles and thrusting arousal against her back while the water sluiced down over them came back to her as clearly as a crystal autumn day.

Her heart began pounding in her chest. "I'm sorry I woke you," she murmured.

"What do you need, Lainie? Are you feeling sick?"

Oh, boy. This was going to be embarrassing. Well, nothing to do now but tell him.

"No. I have a little headache, but otherwise I feel okay. Thanks to you. You did a great job of taking care of a silly drunk last night. I appreciate your efforts."

He waved off her thanks. "No sweat. But if you're not sick, then what did you want to tell me?"

"I, uh, had the oddest nightmare."

"Nightmare? You woke me up to tell me about a dream?"

Yep…embarrassing. "Yes, but I think part of it might be important," she insisted. "Except for…do you have any idea why I would dream about a hummingbird? I don't remember seeing one in the field yesterday."

He arched an eyebrow at her and cleared his throat. "Yeah, I might've seen a hummingbird last night. What about it?" The look in his eyes was clearly irritation, and he folded his arms over his chest.

She shrugged. "Never mind. That's not the important part." This was getting to be more embarrassing by the second. "I also saw my sister in a dream. But she was so miserable and looked so unhappy that she didn't even seem to be the person I know."

Lainie watched him clamp down on his jaw, but he didn't say anything. "The strangest thing was that I was somehow positive that her unhappiness came from this situation with my stalker."

"Do you think your sister's health might've suddenly deteriorated?"

"I don't know. It didn't feel like the misery I saw on her face had anything to do with a physical condition." Lainie hesitated, then said what she feared. "Do you think it's possible that the stalker has kidnapped her in order to get to me?"

"Man. That's really stretching a dream out into a full-fledged movie of the week." Sloan pulled back the covers and swung his legs around to the floor.

Lainie gasped at the sudden move and turned her face in case he was totally naked.

"If it'll make you feel better, we'll go find a pay phone and call the captain to check on things," he said.

She took a chance and peeked out from under her lashes. "Why can't we call from here?" When she saw that he'd worn his jeans to bed, she let out the breath she'd been holding. "And why not on the cell phone?"

"You'd be surprised what things can be traced, Lainie."

Without glancing back toward her, Sloan slipped on one of his new T-shirts. "Get dressed. We've had enough of teaching you how to have fun. It's time we got back to saving your life."

Seven

The town of Edna had disappeared in the rearview mirror long before Sloan managed to get his hormones back under control. With all this raging testosterone and adrenaline, his poor body was taking a beating.

Lainie sat in the passenger seat, eating a bacon and egg taco. She was also balancing a paper cup full of coffee on her jeans-covered left thigh.

It had been all he could do earlier this morning to sit quietly while she'd knelt beside his bed. Watching her talk, with her tousled bed hair and liquid green eyes—so animated and so sexy—had been a painful experience. His body had stirred under the sheets. His muscles had cramped from resisting the urge to draw her up under him.

He hadn't been able to think of anything but making love while those long legs of hers wrapped around his waist. His foremost thought was of driving himself deep inside her, giving them both pleasure for as long as it lasted.

It was a terrible roller coaster of emotions she'd put him on over the last two days. Last night after she'd gone to sleep, he'd sat beside her and stroked her hair, wishing mightily that he could've found a way to spare her the pain of too much alcohol. Sloan felt something shift in his chest when he touched her while she slept. It was something soft, strange and totally foreign. And it made him itchy and restless.

Now all he could think of was that danged hummingbird tattoo on the breast of their hostess last night. At the time Lainie hadn't appeared to notice the tattoo at all. It was unbelievable that she'd dreamed about it.

He couldn't remember having this much trouble with a woman in his entire life.

"Why are we heading in a different direction?" Lainie asked before she popped the last mouthful.

"We're done with backtracking and trying to fool your stalker. There's been no sign of anyone since yesterday at noon. Sequin is only an hour or so north of here, and that's where we're headed."

She choked down her last bite and wadded up the plastic wrapper. "Okay. I guess that's a good idea. I think I'm going to need a nap this afternoon, anyway." Tenderly, she touched her forehead as if the pain was building behind her eyes again.

"Put the trash in that bigger sack there. We'll pitch it out later." He kept an eye on her while she did what he asked. "What did Captain Johnson have to say when you talked to him?"

They'd stopped for gas and food at a convenience store before leaving Edna, and while they were there, Sloan used a pay phone to call in. After a few explanations, the captain had asked to speak to Lainie.

"He didn't say much," she shrugged. "Apparently, he visited with Suzy late last night and learned she was ready to be released from the hospital this morning. She's doing well, he said, and glad to be going home." Lainie turned her head to stare out at the countryside. "She told him she was worried about me."

The miserable note in her voice left Sloan angry and frustrated, but he banked the emotions. "Was the captain going there again this morning?"

"Yes. Jeff was supposed to be taking her home today, but Chet couldn't reach him last night to ask about it."

"Jeff?"

"I told you. My brother-in-law. Suzy's husband."

"Yeah. Right." Sloan didn't know the guy, but as a Ranger, he knew of several things men might think of doing while their wives were off in the hospital. "Well, if Suzy isn't just fine when the captain sees her this morning, he'll find a way to contact us. And I'll turn the cell phone on every hour or two to check for messages. Stop worrying."

She nodded and reached for a CD. "I like the music selection we inherited with this SUV. Mind if I put one on?"

"Nope." But then he remembered the fiasco of yesterday. "Uh...just don't play the one with the honky-tonk song."

She shot him a sideways glare, but the ghost of a

smile played on her lips. "Don't worry. I learned that lesson." The CD she chose began playing, and she turned the sound lower. "But it was fun, wasn't it?"

"Humph." He didn't turn his face, but he could feel her watching his expressions. "I can think of a couple of better ways to have fun."

"Really? That's interesting. What do you do for fun, Ranger Abbott?"

She was putting him on the spot and he squirmed to get in a more comfortable position.

"When I can manage a few days off, I try to get in a little fishing on Canyon Lake or up at Marble Falls. But I haven't had a day off in a long while."

"I know how *that* is," she told him. "Say... where do you live? I've met a few of Chet's Rangers since we moved to Houston. How come I never saw you before?"

"I've been stationed in five Texas cities since I joined the Rangers. I've moved so many times, I mostly just live out of my truck."

"Oh, that must be tough. So...where's home? Where did you grow up?"

He grimaced but kept his eyes on the road. "In Texas."

The incredulous look she shot him bore a hole in the side of his face. "I don't understand."

"My mother was the restless type," he admitted. "Every time we'd get comfortable enough somewhere to call it home, she'd pick up and move us on down the road. I learned a lot about the state of Texas while I was growing up."

"I'll bet you did. But I doubt you learned much about the value of a home and family." Lainie

tsked. ''So was your mother in the service or something?''

''She was a waitress. And a damned good one,''
he added. ''She simply couldn't put down roots. I
always used to wonder why. Now I have a good
idea.''

Lainie raised her eyebrows but didn't ask the obvious question. ''Do I dare ask about your father?
Were your parents divorced?'' she asked instead.

''For most of my life I was convinced that my
father was killed in a car accident when I was two.
It was a nice convenient image.'' Sloan wasn't
thrilled about spilling all his new hurt out for someone else to sort through. He needed to think a little
more before he talked about it.

But Lainie couldn't take the hint and drop the
subject. ''What's different now?'' she probed.

''Everything.'' He reached over and jacked up the
volume, hoping to effectively cut off any more conversation.

Lainie stared at him for a second and then folded
her arms across her chest. With a nod, she turned a
shoulder to him and stared out the window.

Great. Her being mad was a thousand times easier
to handle than having to talk to her about his past.
Man, was she ever a pure pain in the neck. Sloan
wished that the next few days would hurry up and
be done. This forced intimacy was killing him—in
more ways than one.

Just ahead, the scrubby mesquite gave way to tall
oaks. Lainie knew something about pines and oaks
from being raised in Shreveport and nearby eastern

Texas. But the vegetation around here was totally different.

With the windows open, she noticed that the air was getting warmer. Funny, the nights here were cooler than in Houston but the days seemed hotter. Springtime in Texas was kind of an odd mix.

Their tires hummed along the highway, and only occasionally did they pass other cars. The landscape rolled out beside them. Every now and then she'd see a farmhouse.

Wondering about the people who lived there, it thrilled her to catch a glimpse of a car in a driveway or a man on a riding lawnmower. Everything looked so normal, different from what she was used to, but normal nevertheless. Most of the houses had neat yards, flower-filled gardens and swing sets in the back. A few had barns nearby, and once in a while some chickens or a horse could be spotted in a side meadow.

It all seemed homey and so family oriented that Lainie felt jealous. However, she couldn't help but wonder if she'd really be happy living in a big farmhouse with a passel of kids to take care of.

She'd always been perfectly satisfied living in the suburbs, with her parents and sister and her high-profile career. The sudden thought of a husband and children gave her a quick little jitter.

Never before had she taken so much as a moment to think about getting married and having a child. Rocking a baby, watching it grow, wiping its bottom and nose were all things she'd refused to consider. Her parents and sister needed so much attention.

Suzy was the mothering type. Lainie had always taken it for granted that she'd be the aunt and babysitter—not the mother. She'd been so wrapped up in her career, so busy getting ahead and making sure her father was working and her sister had a nice place to live, that she hadn't given a family of her own a second thought.

What would it feel like to be married and give birth to your own child? Would it make you somehow mushy and soft in the head? Or would cradling a baby to your breast and having a toddler lift its arms up to you turn out to be such a wonder that everything else in life would cease to matter?

Lainie blinked back wetness and rubbed at her eyes to clear the blur. The wind and road dust were making her tear up. She slid a glance over at Sloan's profile, wondering what he thought about having kids.

Instantly she turned back to the open window, chastising herself for being an idiot. Know a guy for three days, share one spectacular kiss and a rather intimate time over a toilet bowl, and you start thinking of diapers and baby blankets? That was just the sort of thing she counseled against in her column. She'd told literally hundreds of immature women not to do anything so foolish.

And besides that, she was fairly sure that Sloan had commitment problems. The little he'd told her made it sound as if his mother had been running from an abusive husband, and that's why she couldn't settle down. Lainie had heard those kinds of horror stories all too often.

If it was true, he would be the absolute worst person to dream about. That kind rarely got over their childhood traumas. Good thing the two of them had only shared kisses. Too bad they had been the most spectacular kisses of her lifetime.

She reached over and turned down the music. "How much farther?"

"Gonzales is about ten miles down the road," he told her without looking away from the road. "After that, we cross the Guadalupe, then turn west for another thirty or forty miles."

He stretched in his seat and yawned. "I've never been to this cabin before. But my old buddy, Gabe, gave me directions. It shouldn't be too tough to find."

Sloan threw a curious glance her way. "You've been quiet a long time. What've you been thinking about, Lainie? You trying to figure out who you know that might want to hurt you?"

Shaking her head, she rubbed her palms together, then fiddled with a fingernail. "Just daydreaming." A wash of shame rolled over her and left her irritable and tired.

Instead of working on a possible suspect, she'd been wondering about babies and dream husbands. She decided to concentrate on her current problems and stop making up impossible scenarios in her head.

After they crossed the Guadalupe River bridge and turned away from the midday sun, Lainie started to see some rather interesting farms and a couple of pretty little villages. They passed a Christmas tree farm, then an orchard with beautiful, shady trees. A sign said it was a peach farm. Another sign a little farther down the road advertised "the world's largest pecan" located fifteen miles down the road in Sequin's courthouse square.

The trees alongside the road grew thicker and taller the farther up the river they drove. Soon fishing camps and rustic bed-and-breakfasts sprouted up between the trees.

"This is a beautiful area," Lainie said as they slowed down for a light at a crossroads.

"I'm getting hungry. Mind if we stop at one of these roadside stands?" Sloan turned into a gravel lot beside a vegetable stand that claimed to sell "the world's best peach cobbler."

He idled the SUV and turned to her. "I'll walk over to the country store for some supplies. You go get us a couple of peach cobblers at the outside stand."

"You have all the money."

"Oh, yeah." He dug into his front pocket and pulled out a handful of bills.

Lainie took the money and slammed the door behind her. Sloan grinned as he watched her hips twitching when she walked away. Danged if she wasn't one great package with those long legs and rounded hips snugly swaying in tight new jeans.

He shook his head at his own foolishness. It was just a trick of proximity that was making her seem so important. People didn't come into his life to stay. They came and went, and she would be no different. And that's the way he liked it.

So, all he had to do now was find a way to keep his distance and not give in to the temptation of her rich full lips or the draw of her sexy come-hither eyes. Yeah? Well, he'd give it his best shot, but another night like the last two and all his Ranger training would be of no use.

Twenty minutes later he'd finished shopping and

they downed the last of the cobblers, pitching the paper plates into the trash. He was eager to get to the cabin.

He drove west for a couple of miles, then turned toward the river when he came to the billboard advertising a real estate firm located in San Antonio. But once they'd made that turn everything began to look different. The trees closed in around them, and they passed a couple of shacks that looked more like a border colonia than fishing cabins.

Finally they rounded a bend in the gravel road and came to a dead end. Hell. He must've missed a turn somewhere.

"Look!" Lainie shouted. "Is that the cabin back there through the trees?"

Sloan peered off at the vague outline of a two-story clapboard house. The weeds and bushes had grown up and competed with the low-hanging tree limbs to obscure the view.

He put the SUV into park and unbuckled his seat belt. "Stay here. I'll go check it out and make sure we're in the right place."

"Like hell," she complained as she pulled free of her seat belt and opened the car door. "We're in this together, Ranger Abbott. So, like it or not, I go where you go."

Pushing through the weeds, Sloan led them toward the house. Tree branches scraped their arms and broke with a snap as he shoved them aside for Lainie to follow.

As they got close enough to see the house clearly, he wondered if they were in the right place. The way Gabe had talked about his "cabin" made Sloan think of a rustic fishing shack in the woods. But this was no shack.

Tucked between trees and in the bend of the river, the two-story house looked neat and well cared for. On the left side was the front entry and porch. Closer still, Sloan could see a lane that must serve as a driveway. He'd apparently missed it on their way in. He figured he would go back in a bit and move the SUV.

They headed toward the front door. "Oh, I love this house," Lainie gushed. "Just look at that front porch. It's wonderful."

The long front porch was wide and painted a Federal-blue color. Copper pots containing blue periwinkles sat alongside two white wicker rockers and a short wicker table. Shutters of the same Federal blue adorned each window. And every ground-floor window he could see held a window box full of trailing flowers.

It was all too gingerbready for his taste. But Lainie oohed and aahed as they scanned the side yards. Pointing out a flower and fern garden set among the rocks and trees, she eagerly started up the front stairs.

"Hold it." He gripped her arm and slowed her to a halt. "Let's spend a minute or two checking this out before we rush in. I'm not altogether sure we're in the right place."

She twisted to look up at him. "It's the only house in the vicinity. How will we know?"

Sloan scanned the front door. "There's supposed to be a lock box for the real estate agents."

"I see it!" She pointed to a little metal box attached to the door frame. "This is the place. It has to be."

He tightened his grip on her. "Let's just look around some. It wouldn't hurt to be careful."

They walked around to the side, stepping gingerly across leaves and moss by staying on the stepping stones set in a path. They passed a gardening shed with pots and watering cans stacked neatly beside the door.

A mockingbird screeched suddenly as they neared a lilac bush. "Careful," he told Lainie. "Must be a nest close by. The mother will attack us if she thinks we're a threat."

Checking all the windows for any sign of forced entry, Sloan slowly led them around back. Wind chimes tinkled a cheery sound as they rounded the corner. They came to a patio with a chaise lounge and a glass table with two wrought-iron chairs. Sloan rattled the patio door, but it seemed solidly locked.

Beyond some sparse grass was the river, and the sound of running water could be heard as it crossed over rocks and debris. A small wooden dock jutted out a few feet above the water.

It was too quiet.

"See, there's no one here." Lainie tugged uselessly against the hold he still had on her arm. "It's just like it should be. Can we go in now?"

She could see him evaluating the situation in his head. He mumbled an answer, released her arm and headed back around the house to the front door.

The heat of the day was beginning to seep through the canopy of leaves, and Lainie felt a couple of drops of sweat roll down her neck. Anxious to get inside, both to cool off and get a look at the house's interior, she picked up her steps to keep pace with Sloan. On the outside the place had been decorated like something from a fairy tale. She couldn't wait for a glimpse of what they'd done inside.

Sloan used a combination that he'd been given to make short work of the lock box. Then he used the keys to open the front door.

"Let me go first and check it out," he said as he wiped his brow with his shirtsleeve.

But Lainie ducked under his arm and pushed through the door ahead of him. The place had been secured tightly. No sense standing out here in the heat any longer than necessary.

The living room opened up to their right. It was so homey and tidy that she nearly sighed. An over-stuffed sofa in a Federal-blue print and two side chairs covered in a coordinating solid material looked lived-in and welcoming. The white brick fireplace was raised a few feet and had a brass-and-glass cover. Two lush green ferns stood like senti-nels next to the glass French doors, which led out-side to the patio.

Lainie moved quickly to see the rest of the house, while Sloan methodically checked every closet and nook. The kitchen spread out across the back end of the house. Its wide plank floors gleamed in dark cherry wood, shining against the white cabinets and rough blue-slate counters. White appliances and pale-blue-and-green tiles made the place sunny and welcoming. It was everything a real home should be.

She moved past the breakfast nook, envisioning cozy Sunday mornings with coffee and orange juice, and the comics spread out over the table. Next came the dining room with its round table, big enough for six but set for a candlelight dinner for two.

Flying up the stairs, Lainie ran down the short hall, opening up bedroom and bathroom doors as she went. When she came to the last door, she opened it to discover a master bedroom and bath. The room wasn't as large as the ones in her houses back in Houston, but it was the most compelling room she'd ever beheld.

A gleaming, queen-size brass bed complete with a quilt in various shades of dark blue, a cozy chintz-covered chair and handmade lace curtains all beckoned to weary bodies. Gigantic navy pillows were neatly stacked in a corner next to the whitewashed oak dresser.

Homey. Warm…and safe. Nothing in the world could be very bad as long as they were here in this place. Her stalker and all the trouble back in Houston seemed far, far away and totally unimportant.

Sloan stuck his head through the doorway. "You should've waited. This could easily have been an ambush."

"Oh, isn't it all simply too grand?" she asked, ignoring his comments. "It looks like…like…" She fought to gather her thoughts. "A honeymoon cottage."

He frowned and moved farther into the room. "I think Gabe has rented it out to newlyweds on occasion. Unfortunately, he's been transferred and needs to sell it now." Sloan came around the end of the bed to stand by the window. "You can see the river from here."

Lainie pulled back the curtain, gasping when she saw the full view. "It's incredible."

Sloan laid a hand on her shoulder. "There are better views."

Lainie turned and caught him staring at her. The look in his eyes was intense. She flushed and wanted to look away, but his gaze held her motionless.

He reached out and captured her face in his palm. "You must be exhausted, Lainie." His thumb rubbed lightly under her eye. "Why don't you take a nap while I move the SUV around to the front and bring in the bags?"

The strange rasp in his voice and the narcotic pull of his eyes kept her pinned beneath his hand.

"I…I don't feel tired," she stammered. "Why don't I help you?"

"I can handle it." He slowly dropped his hand to his side. "It'll be better if you make yourself comfortable while I finish checking the grounds."

"But I…"

Backing toward the doorway, Sloan hesitated and cocked his head toward her. "Please, Lainie. Relax and let me handle it, just this once."

He disappeared down the hall without waiting for her reply. What had that look been all about? She'd barely heard a word he'd said. The electric jolts from his gaze and from his touch were still zinging through her body. She'd swear it was the most sensual and erotic few moments she had ever spent, and it left her weak-kneed and tongue-tied.

Needing to throw some cold water on her overheated face, Lainie turned toward the bathroom. But the gorgeous view from the open window caught her attention midstride.

The clear, blue sky was peeking through the light green leaves of the tallest trees. This was springtime at its finest, she was sure. The warm sun shone through the glass, gently lulling her with its soft promise.

Lainie just had to get out into the lush gardens so she could listen to the birds and to the tinkling ripples of the river over the rocks. What a place this was. Sloan had brought them to the perfect spot. All the bad things that had happened back in Houston could never touch her here.

It only took her a minute or two to bound down the stairs and then dash out the back door into the garden. Taking a deep, cleansing breath of springtime air, Lainie began to really relax. The birds were squawking above her and butterflies flitted here and there amongst the flowers.

She lifted her head to feel the sun on her face when she suddenly spotted a small deer taking a drink from the river. How adorable. And how peaceful it looked there.

Wondering whether she could get nearer for a better view, she stepped into the stand of trees between them and eased closer to the river. The deer raised its head and sniffed the air, then swished its tiny white tail and bounded down the riverbank.

Lainie rushed after it, trying to keep it within sight. As she was just about to run out of breath, she spotted a fisherman wading in the shallows. The quick turn of her head to see who was there cost her the deer. In that instant it was gone.

"Hello there," the man with the pole and wading boots called to her. He had on a red-checked flannel shirt with the sleeves rolled up and a black baseball cap that covered his eyes.

"Hi. Did you just see that deer?" she asked.

"Just now? No. But the woods are full of White-Tails this time of year. It isn't hunting season and they know they're safe."

"Do you live around here?" Lainie moved toward the water, fascinated by the man's rod and reel. It was very long and the tip whipped every time he moved his wrist.

"I'm renting a cabin downstream for a couple of weeks." He looked over her shoulder at the house and nodded to it. "You own this place?"

She opened her mouth to tell him no, when she heard something rustle in the bushes behind her. Before she turned to check it out, she saw the stranger's eyes widen and a quick glimpse of something like fear flicked over his features.

While the man stood speechless, Sloan appeared from behind a tree, captured her in his arms and hugged her in a tight embrace. "There you are, sweetheart. I've been looking all over."

Lainie tried to pull away, but Sloan held her arms pinned against her side. She couldn't move. But she could open her mouth, and she was about to ask Ranger Abbott if he'd lost his ever-loving mind.

"Sloan, what—"

He cupped the back of her head and pushed her face into his chest, effectively cutting off her words—and her air.

"Howdy, neighbor," Sloan called to the stranger. "Sorry if my wife disturbed your cast. We're new-lyweds, you know, and I'm afraid we've had our first spat."

Newlyweds? Spat? She squirmed in his embrace, but he tightened his hold.

"Ah…no problem. She was chasing a deer," the fisherman told him.

"She was trying to get me to chase her," Sloan drawled. "But my parents will be here in a few minutes for a visit, and as much as I'd rather play in the woods with my new wife, I'm afraid we have to get the house straightened out instead."

"Oh. I see. Well, don't let me stop you," the man said.

She pushed hard against Sloan's chest and finally pulled free of him. "What…" she managed before he dropped his mouth over hers.

Stunned, she grabbed hold of his shirt and hung on for dear life. Forgetting about the fisherman watching them and about being furious with Sloan for manhandling her, she abandoned all thought and gave herself up to the kiss. Swirling heat from the press of his lips and the brush of his tongue shimmered over her skin.

Without breaking contact, Sloan picked her up in his arms and headed back up the bank toward the house. In a few minutes they were on the front porch, and he set her down to open the door. He still held on to her with one arm tightly around her waist.

"Are you crazy?" she yelped as she drew in a deep breath.

"No, I was trying to be your bodyguard." He kicked open the door, picked her up again and then slammed the door shut behind them. "Now I have something else in mind."

He headed for the stairs.

"Put me down," she squeaked. Sloan had obviously lost his mind. A shiver of danger rocked through her.

"Not yet," he growled as he took the stairs two at a time.

"Put me down this…"

He shoved his way into the master bedroom and dropped her onto the bed with enough force to knock the words right out of her.

"…instant," she finished with a whoosh of air.

"Do you ever shut up?" he asked, then sat down on the edge of the bed and gathered her up in his arms.

"But…wait a minute," she sputtered.

"This time I'm in charge," he whispered, and bent closer to her lips. "Next time it'll be your turn."

He chuckled at her surprised look. Then he effectively made sure she understood his intentions by once again covering her mouth with his own.

Eight

Sloan broke the kiss, trying to find the strength to put some distance between them and not do what his body demanded. But looking down at her made him nearly frantic to kiss her again. Lainie leaned back on the bed, smiling up at him—just as he'd dreamed for every moment of the past forty-eight hours.

The sexy look on her face was erotic as hell. Her bedroom eyes were almost closed and her breathing was none too steady. His own was ragged and rough. He was dazzled by her.

He wanted to explore every inch of her, find every sensitive crevice and hidden tender spot. In a way it felt as if he already knew everything about her, as though he'd stripped her so many times in his thoughts that he was familiar with her most minute cell. And yet, the sense of a new adventure was ripening in his gut.

He'd wanted this—and fought it—for two days now, and had finally come to the breaking point. The fragile strings of his control were stretched thin. Not sure he had the patience and the fortitude to make everything right for her, he bit down on the inside of his cheek until it hurt, in order to slow down. Heaven help him, the aching hunger had turned into an urgent, stabbing pain.

He lifted his hand to gently graze the line of her jaw with a knuckle. So much like silken porcelain.

"Lainie," he managed through a shaky voice.

Her eyes were closed and she didn't move. He wasn't too sure she'd heard him. "Lainie," he began again a little louder. "I know I said this was my turn but…if you don't want the same thing I do…if I've read you wrong…please tell me to stop. In another few minutes it will be too late to go back."

She finally opened her eyes to languidly scrutinize him. "If I didn't want it, I wouldn't be here, Sloan." Then with a Mona Lisa smile, she tilted her head. "You're a man of action. Just shut up and kiss me."

"It's my show, sweetheart." Drawing courage from her words, he picked up her hand and slowly, hungrily, nibbled on her fingertips. Licking the knuckles, kissing each tip, he tasted peaches and cream. Yes, just as he'd known he would. Every single inch tasted sweet…and turned him on.

She made a small sound—part shock, part need. Watching him with those big, luminous, green eyes, she ran her tongue over her lips. It was his total undoing. A mere sliver of a thought about protection for them raced through his mind, and he was glad he'd been bold enough to buy it when they'd stopped.

Sloan had to sample more before he lost every last semblance of integrity and ravaged her. The savage demands of his body were already ruling his mind. Pressing his lips to the sensitive inside of her wrist, he stopped there to taste, and felt her pulse jump. The sensation sent electric vibrations down his body where they flirted with the throbbing reverberations of his own pulse.

He kept his gaze locked with hers as he licked his way up her arm. She fisted her hand and moaned when he found the next tender spot on the inside of her elbow.

Excitement and urgency pushed past his control and spiraled throughout his body, spreading smoke and flame. He let his tongue linger on the soft skin, moistening, nipping, cherishing. And he found himself fighting the urge to gobble her whole.

Her eyelids drooped and she tried to speak. "Sloan…" But whatever else she'd wanted to say was lost to a whimpered moan.

He didn't lift his mouth, but his free hand slid up her thigh, around her hip to her waist, then under her T-shirt to the small of her back. When he reached her warm and silky bare skin, she arched up to him.

Her eyes slowly opened again, and he saw only wide fathomless passion staring back at him. It was too much. No more teasing. Whatever minimal control he'd had was lost.

He breathed a whispered curse, then jerked her shirt up and over her head. She gasped at the brash movement. He leaned her back again and her legs instinctively fell open. He quickly shoved his thigh between her knees for balance.

Bending to her, he crushed her mouth under his. He let his tongue mimic other actions, sliding in and out, tangling with hers in a frantic embrace. Lainie groaned and flexed her body, sending pleasure coiling deep within him.

Sloan released her mouth to cruise down her chin, heading for the satiny gratification of her neck. Moving lower, he found her collarbone with his tongue and teeth, licking, sucking and nibbling, until he felt the beat of a pulse at the base of her neck.

Sobbing out his name, she grabbed his shoulders and hung on, while his hands moved up her rib cage and cradled her small, firm breasts. He suddenly craved nothing more than pleasing her. Driving her as crazy with wanting as he was.

''Sloan, please,'' she pleaded.

Yes, he wanted to please them both. If only this primeval demand to make sure she was with him would keep him together long enough.

Using his teeth to shove aside her bra straps, he licked his way down the swell of her breasts. His thumbs flicked against her nipples and found the hardened tips right through the silky material still clinging to her. She arched again, pushing hard where his thumbs teased.

At last he used his fingers to push the material down and away, desperate to put his mouth where his hands had been. That gave him free rein to open his mouth over one tight nipple. Breathing out a hot, humid breath over her sensitive skin, he watched the tip pucker even tighter.

The temptation was stronger than the need to go slow so he let himself taste, licking, ringing the tip and giving them both the pleasure of intimate physical contact. At the same time he used his free hand to massage her thigh, kneading his way to the tender inside and on up to her core. When he closed his mouth fully over her breast, he also pressed down with the heel of his hand, feeling tension at the juncture of her jeans.

Lainie bucked against his hand and moaned. ''Oh, please. Please,'' she begged. ''Stop teasing and make love to me.''

He grinned when he heard the same desperation in her voice that he was feeling. ''My turn. My call,'' he drawled like a man who knew what he was doing.

But sweat beaded on his forehead from the sheer effort of control. He managed to leash his fierce desire and concentrated on bringing her to the edge and back instead. He slowly slid down her jeans zipper, then she helped him pull her legs free.

Anchoring her tightly against him, he bent to take the other nipple in his mouth while drawing his fingers lightly up the inside of her thigh and under the elastic of her panties. His thumb threaded through the wiry curls he found there and sought out the hidden pearl at the heart of her desire.

Dampness and warmth flooded his fingers as he flicked his tongue over her nipple at the same time he rubbed his thumb over her nub of pleasure. She gasped and went rigid for a moment, then seemed to melt under him.

He was undone by the shudders that rocked her, fascinated by the rawness of passion that he saw on her face. Pressing her back against the pillows, Sloan made short work of his own clothes and finished tugging her free of the bra.

She opened her eyes and reached out to touch him. "Patience, sweetheart," he advised shakily as he held back her hands. Though he felt no patience of his own, he tried to soothe her by stroking the smooth skin on her belly.

He'd been shocked and blown away by the abandonment and ecstasy he'd seen written on her face as she'd reached a climax. Satisfying her every erotic desire before he satisfied himself suddenly became the most important mission he'd ever taken on.

Tasting her breasts again gave them both pleasure. Nipping. Pulling. Suckling. She drove her fingers through his hair, massaging his scalp as she moaned with ferocious joy. He moved lower, nipping and laving the tender skin underneath her breasts, then licking his way down to her belly button.

He circled it with kisses, dipping and swirling over the sensitive flesh. Erotic hunger and simple desperation drove him into a frenzy. Moving lower still, he placed warm, wet kisses through the silky material until she was jerking under him once again.

Finally, he hooked a finger under her elastic waistband and tugged, trying to remove the last impediment, the one torturing them both. The flimsy material ripped apart, and he quickly pitched it aside.

She gasped and laughed breathlessly at his impatience and the surprising sound the material made when it tore. But she stiffened when he bent to continue his openmouthed journey. With lips and teeth, he explored her mound.

His tongue sank into the dark crevice between her thighs. Whimpering again, she squirmed, giving him a free path to her core. He palmed her naked thighs and delighted in running his thumbs up and down the delicate skin there.

Another moan filled the air, but this time he wasn't sure whether it was hers or his. Complete control of her body, the ability to drive her up and then back down, thrilled him beyond word or thought. He wanted to drag it on forever, but he knew his time was growing short.

He planted a gentle, lingering kiss in the most secret of her places and she groaned, arching her lower back. The movement left her wide open to him and he drove his tongue deep inside her.

She shrieked, jerked her hips and tensed against him. He could feel the drumbeat of pulses starting deep inside her so he hauled himself up her body, biting and nibbling the velvet skin in his path. Stroking and fondling her sweat-slickened body, he ran his tongue around both her breasts before he took her mouth with a deep plunging kiss.

"Now, please, Sloan," she rasped against his lips. Her voice was taut, thin, desperate. "You're making me crazy. I have to…I must." The tension written on her face told him more than the words.

"Soon," he whispered. He quickly reached for his jeans, ripped the condom he'd bought from his pocket and rolled it over himself in two seconds flat.

He was past all restraint as he braced his hands on either side of her head and thrust into the heavenly, wet passage that led to her core. Tight, hot and pulsating, the sensations assailed him.

Sloan was stunned to find the first place he'd ever really thought of as home.

The bewitching woman below him stared up at him with glazed eyes. Breathing short little gasps through her mouth, she jerked her hips upward, driving him deeper. He stilled, wanting to experience all the sensations he found inside her. But it was pure torture.

Sloan took one last stab at coherence and fairness before he went totally mad. "Are you okay?"

"No." Another intoxicated and bold smile graced her lips. "And if you don't finish this right now, I swear you're a dead man, Sloan Abbott."

That was the last thing he heard before she undulated her hips once again and the waves of passion inside her tore the last bit of sense from him. He could only pump and buck against the pressure and heat as her internal muscles held him, sucked him up and rolled against him.

Finally—home.

Somewhere in a distant fog, he heard her screams of pleasure. And at last, he felt her crashing tide of hot lava burning them both, while he could do nothing but shout and shatter in one huge, drawn-out explosion of his own.

When Lainie came to her senses, Sloan was collapsed on top of her. It was the most intimate, the most comfortable position she'd ever been in.

She held on and tried to remember how to breathe. She loved being this close to him. If it had been possible, she would've built herself a nest right beside him so she would never have to leave.

Sloan gathered her up and rolled on his back. She lay sprawled out over him, and felt the erratic beating of his heart next to hers. Planting a whisper of a kiss against his sweat-slickened neck, she tried to think past the pounding in her ears.

In her entire twenty-eight years, she'd never known…had never realized what being with the right man would be like. How could she have ever imagined that something so irreversible would happen to her with this one man?

As fatalistic and as impetuous as it sounded, Sloan would be the last man she ever made love to. In her gut, in her soul, she knew it was true.

Lainie didn't want it to be so. Didn't want to love him. If she'd had the slightest hint that her feelings would be this intense, she never would've let things get out of hand. But making love with him had seemed so inevitable. As certain as breathing air.

She shut her eyes and moaned quietly. What had she done to herself? She should've known better than to trust her emotions when everything was so turned around in her life. Something inside her had changed forever.

Sloan was a loner. A man with no ties and no inclination to ever have any. Exactly the wrong kind of guy to fall in love with. A lonely miserable existence—loving a man who couldn't love her in return stretched out in her imagination.

She tried to sit up but Sloan held her to his chest with both arms. "Don't leave yet," he murmured as he brushed a kiss over her shoulder. "That was amazing.'' He sounded as stunned as she felt. ''You are incredible, Lainie.''

''Really?'' Her face warmed with pleasure at the compliment. ''I wasn't sure you...thought of me that way. After all, we hardly know each other.''

''I thought of you *that* way the first time I laid eyes on you. And I figured maybe you thought we knew each other a little too well after last night.''

''Mmmm,'' she groaned as she planted a kiss on his chest. ''Yeah. I guess this was destined to be.''

''You don't sound so sure. Are you having second thoughts?'' He twisted his head to search her eyes.

''No. No regrets.'' She reached out to touch his lips, running her fingertip lightly over the swollen flesh. ''I may feel a tiny bit guilty, however. I don't normally jump into the sack with a guy I've only known for two days, Texas Ranger or not.''

''Want to pretend that it never happened and go back to being bodyguard and damsel in distress?'' His eyes glinted with wary hesitation as he pressed a kiss to her temple.

''No. We couldn't go back now...even if we wanted to.'' No matter what the future held for them, she wouldn't have missed this time with him for anything.

He chuckled under her and the movement awakened a stir of need that skittered along her spine. ''I want you to know that I meant it when I said the next time would be your turn.'' He stroked her hair away from her face, then ran his fingers lightly across her back. ''Just don't wait too long.''

''You're kidding.'' She laughed lightly at the surprising thought. But she felt him growing hard against her belly. How could she want him this much again, knowing that sex would be all they'd ever have?

He tensed and lifted his head to gaze into her eyes. "Too soon for you? I mean…are you too sore? Too hungry? Too tired?"

Her shameless, wanton body betrayed her as he kindled a wildfire in her center. There would be no more sensible thoughts for tonight. She rotated her hips against his and lifted up on both arms to stare into his eyes. "Does that feel too tired to you, Ranger Abbott?"

He slid his hands to her hips, lifting her as she slowly fitted herself down on his shaft. She felt as if fire raced over her skin and danced through her veins. But it felt weirdly perfect. Luscious, decadent and…complete.

She raised up slowly, and he thrust deeper, higher, making her tighten and tremble with desire. Watching his face, gazing into his intense brown eyes, she rode him with pure abandon.

Sloan petted and stroked her breasts, bent double and took each tip into his mouth. She felt the pull deep in her womb as he suckled.

Using his hands and mouth, he brought her to the brink over and over. Then he slowed down the pace, tightly restraining her movements as she sat astride him.

Not able to stand any more, she rose above him. Finding her senses, then losing them once more, she mindlessly pumped down over him. Too soon she felt the shudder rolling through her as he drove himself deep inside for one last thrust. They held on to each other as they once again exploded over the brink, then collapsed together into ecstatic oblivion.

*   *   *

Sloan awoke to bright sunshine and a lonely bed. When he'd reached over to draw Lainie to him as he'd done throughout the night, his hands touched only cool, wrinkled sheets.

At first he panicked and sat straight up in bed. Was something wrong? Had he lost himself so completely that Lainie's stalker had drawn her away from his side?

Then he heard the shower running. He collapsed back against the pillows and expelled the breath he'd been holding.

Thank God.

The whole basis for his life up to now lay in tatters before him. And he was so bewitched by Lainie that he couldn't even begin to figure out why.

Up until last night, he'd hoped that a good roll in the hay would rid him of the unusual tenderness he'd been feeling toward her.

As tough as she talked, and as strong as she appeared on the outside, when she looked at him, all he could see in her face were picket fences and scores of babies. She was family oriented, even if her family wasn't perfect. And families were the absolute last thing he'd ever imagined he'd be interested in.

But he was interested in her. The way her eyes lit up when she talked about learning to have fun. The determination he saw when she talked about her work. The softness he'd spied in her face when she looked at him.

All this time he'd thought they were exact opposites. Now he wondered if that was really true.

Nothing about the two of them made much sense at the moment. Except...now that he knew what it felt like to have her explode in his arms, he could never go back to the way they'd been before.

Maybe they would still go back to their own worlds when this whole thing blew over, but his life would be forever changed. And in the meantime, she'd be in his bed and in his arms until the stalker was caught.

From the bathroom, he heard a sudden high-pitched squeal. He threw the covers off and headed toward the closed door.

Knocking loudly, then bursting into the room without waiting for an answer, he didn't know what to expect. "Lainie? What's the matter?"

"What? I sure hope that's you, Sloan. I can't hear you clearly with the water running."

He peeked around a shower curtain that was decorated with navy blue and yellow fish. She stood under the spray as water poured over her soapy body. The suds were everywhere, in her hair, sluicing down the curves of her body and disappearing into cracks and crevices he had only just visited himself.

Instantly aroused and desperate for her, he stepped into the shower stall behind her. "I thought something was wrong. Why did you scream?"

Lainie turned to face him. "What are you doing in here? What's the matter with you?" She fought to clear the soap from her eyes so she could see him.

He couldn't believe he was this hungry for her again after their spectacularly long night. The sight of her made his heart race as he reached out to pull her close.

"I thought you were in trouble. You screamed," he said once he was holding her slippery body in his arms.

"I did not scream." She twisted against his chest and the soap bubbles covered him. "The shampoo bottle dropped and landed on my foot. Besides, I never scream."

"Wanna bet?" He drew in a lungful of strawberry scent, coming from the soap that now covered them both. "I bet I can make you scream in the next few minutes."

He ran his hand over her hot, smooth skin. She was wet and slick and driving him wild.

She put her hands on his shoulders for support as he crushed his mouth down over hers. Gasping and sputtering in shock, she reared back and gazed into his eyes with such a passionate need that it took him by surprise.

"Hang on, sweetheart." He turned her around and braced her against the tile. Sliding his hands down her hips, he lifted her bottom. "Put your arms around my neck."

Lainie instinctively slid her long legs around him, and he entered her with one swift thrust. She tightened her legs, digging her nails into his shoulders at the same time. Water beat against his back, the spray becoming cooler as his skin burned with the fire of desire.

"Sloan…now…please…now."

He felt her muscles tighten and he rammed deeper yet, bending his head to take the tip of her breast in his mouth. She dug her fingers into his scalp and bit down on his shoulder.

"Come on, Lainie," he urged. "Let go. It's all right. I'm here to catch you."

Her shudder began like a crest of a wave and moved into him. He groaned, thrusting one last time.

And as he followed her over the edge, her screams of climax rang in his ears…and warmed his soul.

Nine

"**H**mm. Feed me." She was stretched out next to Sloan on the unmade bed, luxuriating in the tingling fog she'd been lazing in since their stupendous shower.

"What would you like to eat?" Sloan winked at her. With a wide smile, he rolled over on his side and leaned up on an elbow. He lightly ran a fingertip down between her breasts, giving her the chills.

Grinning, Lainie sat up on the side of the bed with her back to him, trying to gain a little distance from the temptation to fall back into his arms. "Real food, please. I need sustenance. You're absolutely wonderful. But I can't keep up with you without solid food."

The thought of touching him and having him touch her again made her tingle all over. No matter how exhausted she was or how consumed and satiated she felt, she didn't think she would ever get too much of Sloan.

"Well, if that's the case..." She felt the mattress rise as he rolled off his side of the bed. "How about eggs and toast?"

"And coffee?" She twisted around to watch him as he drew a pair of jeans up his long body and over his tight butt.

He left the button and the zipper down while he rummaged around looking for a shirt. "Definitely coffee."

He was so beautiful. She could sit and watch him all day long. His movements were precise and athletic. With his broad shoulders and muscular arms, he looked as if he lifted weights. On the other hand, Lainie couldn't imagine Sloan wasting time in a gym.

Slipping his arms through the sleeves of the shirt he'd found, Sloan strode into the master bathroom, leaving the shirt unbuttoned. The sound of running water bubbled out from the still-open door. She quickly found something to put on. Sliding her own arms into the see-through sleeves of her mother's idea of a robe, she strolled over to ask him another question.

Leaning back against the doorjamb, she folded her arms across her chest. "Where'd we get eggs, bread and coffee?"

He was in the process of slathering his face with soap. "I bought supplies yesterday at the roadside market." Smiling into the mirror at her, he picked up a razor. "I brought them in and put them away while you were busy making small talk with that suspicious fisherman."

"Suspicious? Oh, really?" She narrowed her eyebrows and lowered her chin, waiting for a fight. "In my opinion, that man was a perfectly legitimate neighbor who happens to like to wade for fish in the river."

"I see. And you arrived at this enlightened opinion because you have so much experience with what, fishing?"

She stepped closer so she could face him squarely in the mirror. "I've never been fishing. But he was certainly dressed for it. And he was holding a rod and reel."

Sloan screwed up his mouth and drew the razor blade down one cheek. "Uh-huh. So I guess it wouldn't matter that he didn't have a lure tied to the end of his line?"

The heat from his back through his shirt drew her closer still. "I don't know. I'm not sure what a lure is used for. But the man seemed nice enough."

Sloan barked out a quick laugh. "Maybe while we're here I'll give you a fishing lesson." Quieting down and raising his chin, he made short work of shaving his neck. "That is, after I spend a little time scouting out where that guy came from and where he went," he told her when he'd put down the razor.

Spying her own image and the tangled mess of her half-dried hair in the mirror over his shoulder, Lainie decided she didn't need that particular view right now. So she put her hands under the tails of his shirt, slid them around his waist and leaned her cheek against his back. "Why, Ranger Abbott, I do believe that sounds like a date. Are you asking me to accompany you for a fishing lesson? Would we have a picnic, too?" She drawled the words out in her best Louisiana accent. Sliding her hands up his chest, then digging them through the curly hair there, she felt the muscles bunch and jerk under her fingers.

In the next instant he spun around and had her in his arms. "You little tease. I can't think straight when you're this close." His face still carried remnants of soap, lingering here and there. But all Lainie found when she looked was the hard glint of passion in his eyes.

Brushing his lips across hers, he arched her over his arm and pressed her closer to his heart. She felt her nipples hardening against the solid plane of his chest. The blood began to pump furiously through her own heart, skipping lightly along her veins.

He rained hot kisses past her mouth and down her throat. Then his hand moved under her robe and settled over one breast. Lainie could smell the citrusy scent of his shaving cream and felt the pull begin deep inside her belly. She pushed her hips against his and twisted one leg around his thigh, trying to get closer.

But at that very moment her stomach growled.

Sloan lifted his head and stood her up solidly on two feet. "Sounds like you're hungry for something entirely different than I am, sweetheart." His voice was raspy and hoarse, but he managed to take a step back. "I guess I'd better feed you before we end up spending the entire day in bed. I wouldn't want you to starve while I'm supposed to be on guard and protecting your life."

Her head was spinning, and Lainie could feel the pink sting of embarrassment riding up her neck.

Sloan turned back to the sink and splashed water over his face.

His little time-out from her looked like something she should be doing, as well. Cold water wouldn't be a cure for what she wanted, however.

She crept out of the bathroom and headed for one of her open suitcases. She had to get dressed before her body went totally out of control and she jumped him.

She'd never watched a man shave before. It had seemed so intimate, so erotic, as he'd glided the sharp blade back and forth over his skin. Breathlessly she grabbed up a pair of jeans and a shirt—and her brush—trying to push the images and the sexy sensations into the background of her mind.

The past twelve hours with him had been so familiar and close that she desperately needed to regain her senses. When the police finally captured her stalker and this whole business was over, Sloan would be on his way. He obviously had an important errand that had caused him to take a leave from the Rangers, and she was sure he wanted to get back to it as soon as possible. By then, she would be back to her real life, her job and her family.

The illusion of intimacy between them was just that—an illusion.

Several times she'd thought about telling him she loved him, now that she'd come to that conclusion. At odd moments she'd wanted to shout it out to whoever would listen. Just imagine—someone like her could actually fall in love for the first time. That was big news.

But Lainie wasn't fool enough to actually tell Sloan that she loved him. A man so afraid of commitment would run for the hills if he had any idea of her feelings. And she wanted every minute with him that she could steal.

He came out of the bathroom, tucking his shirt into his jeans. Reaching for his boots, he threw her a quick glance.

"The bathroom's all yours. I'll start the coffee."

As he disappeared around the corner, she heaved a sigh and prepared to do battle with the brilliant-red rat's nest that was her hair. She intended to be presentable for what was left of her rapidly disappearing time with Sloan.

Sloan dropped a couple of slices of bread into the toaster. He caught himself absently humming that idiotic tune about honky-tonk bars again, smiling to himself when it made him think about Lainie. He couldn't think of another woman who'd invaded his thoughts so often.

Her zest for life. Her zeal to learn. She was irritable and touchy, yet sensitive and fun. He'd never seen anyone who could heat up as fast, nor anyone who could blush so easily.

She was an amazing miracle that had stampeded her way into his life and under his skin.

"I can smell the coffee brewing." Lainie swung into the kitchen and headed for the coffeepot. "Is it ready?"

"Yes, ma'am. Fetch a mug from that cupboard. The eggs will be ready shortly."

Lainie filled a cup, took a sip, then slowly turned to watch him scramble the eggs. "Ma'am? Fetch?" she mimicked. "Well, aren't you just the cutest cowpoke on the block, Ranger Abbott.'' She leaned against the counter and batted her eyelashes at him.

''You want to make fun, or would you rather not eat your eggs out of the garbage?''

''Oops. Sorry.'' She hung her head contritely and sat down at the breakfast table. ''But you really are the most Texas-oriented man I've ever met.'' She put her hands palms out in front of her face. ''Not that I mind. In fact, I think it's wonderful.''

Sloan put both their plates on the table, grabbed his mug and sat down. ''I've always thought of myself as a pure Texan, born and bred. Even spent summers working on cattle ranches and spent some time on the rodeo circuit.'' He took a bite of egg, swallowed and decided to go ahead and say what was on his mind. ''I just recently discovered I wasn't born in Texas. My father was raised in Illinois and I was born in Chicago.''

''You just recently discovered that? What about your birth certificate? You have to have a birth certificate to get into school.''

He let himself frown at the memory. ''Apparently, my mother bought a phony birth certificate for me from some guy she knew. My name isn't even Abbott. That's phony, too.''

''Why would she do such a thing?'' Lainie asked. ''Was she trying to hide from an abusive husband?''

He shook his head. ''No, it was more like abusive in-laws, I think. She desperately wanted to keep our real identities hidden.''

''I'm sorry, Sloan. It has to be tough to learn that kind of thing after you're an adult. What do you think about it?'' She took a bite of toast and waited for him.

He just wished he knew what *she* really thought about a guy who didn't even know his own name. But she was in her psychologist-advisor mode and unreadable at the moment. "I don't know yet," he admitted. "I've been trying not to think about it a whole hell of a lot." Every time he did, his stomach turned and his skin crawled.

"Does this have something to do with your leave of absence from the Rangers?"

Well, he was doomed to talk about it now. Might as well lay the whole thing out for her. She was the first person who would know the whole story, and he wondered how the knowledge would affect her.

Pushing aside his plate and downing the last swallow of coffee, he took a second to think of how to begin. "You remember I told you that my mother died a couple of months ago?"

Lainie nodded and kept her eyes trained on his.

"When I went to her apartment to clear out her things a few days later, I found a letter addressed to me in a dresser along with some other papers." The chair he'd been sitting in suddenly became too hard to sit in any longer so he got up and paced to the window. "It was a confession of sorts. And also what I guess you would call a deathbed request."

Standing, Lainie picked up their dishes and went to the sink. He knew she was watching him closely, even though he had his back to her most of the time. But she didn't interrupt, and never made a sound.

Clearing his throat, a scratchy one that had suddenly become dry and rough, he began, "My father wasn't killed in any car accident when I was two. That was all a big lie. He was sent to prison."

Lainie's eyes grew wide, then softened. But she still didn't say anything, so he continued.

"Apparently, my father's parents were rather well-to-do. They hadn't thought my mother was good enough for their son when they'd first married. So when my father was tried and sentenced to prison for raping and murdering a friend of Mother's, they blamed her for having friends that were no good."

"Oh, Sloan. How horrible for your poor mother." He could see the sympathy written on her face, but he wasn't sure that's what he wanted to see there.

He liked the look of passion and the secret loving glances Lainie usually gave him. But pity was something he'd never wanted from anyone, least of all from her.

"Yes, well…maybe." He looked away. "Anyway, I guess my grandparents hired an attorney to fight Mother over custody of me after my father was sent away. They claimed she was unfit to raise a child.

"My mother was poor, an uneducated orphan from Texas," he continued. "She panicked and fled back to where she was raised. Mother changed our last name, then kept moving us around the state, hoping to stay ahead of the authorities. She was positive her in-laws would've hired private investigators to find us, so she stayed away from any old friends or places she'd known in her youth."

Lainie ran water over the dishes in the sink, then dried her hands. "Her letter must've been impossibly hard for you to read. Whatever became of your father?"

He shrugged a shoulder and tried to sound unaffected. "I don't know. Mother didn't bother to find out. She ran away and never looked back."

"She must've carried a lot of guilt about that all those years." Lainie's voice was sympathetic and kind, but that was the last thing he wanted. "Did she believe he was guilty?"

"What?"

"Did your mother think her husband had really raped and murdered her friend?"

Sloan hadn't thought about that problem yet. "I don't know that either. She didn't say in her letter." Sloan moved to a chair and spun it backward so he could sit and lean his elbows on the high back. "Thinking about it now, I guess she must've believed he was innocent or she wouldn't have asked me to try to find him."

"She did?"

"Yes. That's the request I mentioned. She told me his name and asked me to try to locate him after all these years."

Lainie nodded and quietly sat down in a chair opposite him. "How do you feel about that?" she asked slowly.

He didn't want to think about this now, and a blue haze of panic instantly clouded his eyes. "Dammit, woman! Quit with the psychoanalyzing, will you?" He swung his leg over the seat and stood as the chair went flying. "I didn't tell you about all of this just so you could give me advice or feel sorry for me."

"Why did you tell me?"

He couldn't think, couldn't stop the sudden rolling in his stomach or the tension from closing in around him. "I'll be danged if I know." He paced to the window, feeling like he'd been sentenced to a cell himself.

Looking out the window, Sloan thought of his boss and the reason he was tied to Lainie in the first place. "I have to go out. I want to check on where that guy from yesterday is staying, and I need to call the captain from a pay phone away from this location."

He turned to face her and saw brilliant green eyes shrouded in a blank stare. "I'll leave you my two-way pager, so you can contact me if anybody shows up here," he hedged. "I think you'll be safe enough, but stay in the cabin. Okay?"

She didn't look up at him, but kept her eyes trained on a toast crumb on the table.

"This is important, Lainie. It might mean your life or death. Promise me."

She stood, but looked unruffled in the face of his demand. "Stop worrying about me. I'll be fine."

Frustrated that he'd had to admit a past he knew nothing about, and with his nerves back on that raw edge, Sloan stomped around the cabin until he was ready to go. If the fool woman managed to get herself killed because she couldn't follow his orders, he would damn well wring her neck when he got back.

Shell-shocked from Sloan's sudden change and unable to think straight, Lainie silently locked all the doors behind him and headed upstairs to take a nap. Her body ached in places she didn't know existed, and she could barely keep her eyes open for lack of sleep. But when she reclined back against the pillows, instead of sleep, images of Sloan and echoes of the words he'd said came back to devil her.

She wasn't certain what had happened to cause his sudden anger. Things seemed to be going well while he'd been discussing his background. She'd never felt closer to anyone in her whole life.

Then came the flash of rage. She wanted to focus on what his actions might've meant. What they could tell her about his feelings.

Using raw instincts and her training in problem solving, Lainie began to piece together some possibilities. She was positive he felt something for her. The tender way he looked at her and the sensitive way he'd made love told her that much.

She was sure a man like Sloan would never talk about his past to someone he didn't really trust. And the fact that his father was in prison seemed to embarrass him. If he didn't feel close to her, Lainie knew he would've stayed silent about that.

So he did care.

But when she'd tried to probe his deeper feelings, he'd exploded. A sudden rage like that was normally a cover for the fear that something or someone was getting too close. Was that it? Had he felt trapped by her?

Maybe it was his way of keeping his distance. Or of reminding her that their days together were numbered and not to get too close. Perhaps he'd unexpectedly remembered his mission and responsibility to the Rangers.

Whatever it was that had broken into one of the closest personal interchanges she'd ever experienced, she wished that they could find a path back to that feeling of togetherness.

All of a sudden, Lainie was lost again. This was another one of those times when she really needed to talk things over with her sister. Suzy had always been her lifeline. She could tell her anything…and did. They'd talked over every move she'd ever made in her life.

A hazy vision of her dream from the other day, where Suzy was sobbing uncontrollably, came to mind. It made Lainie stop short. Had she really been so unthinking as to imagine that her sister was happy when she was really miserable?

Giving Sloan the control during their lovemaking and discovering that she cared about him had shifted all her perspectives. Now she had the uncomfortable feeling that perhaps she was really a selfish and controlling witch who didn't care about anyone else's troubles.

Was it true? Had she been so wrapped up in her problems that she'd neglected the things that were the most important?

The world began to shift under her. She'd called Suzy in the hospital the other day from that pay phone in the ladies' room at the roadside café to check on her physical well-being. But even then Lainie hadn't asked her sister how she was doing emotionally. She'd been so full of her own flight into the countryside with the sexy Texas Ranger that she hadn't let Suzy get a word in edgewise.

Lainie eyed the white bedside phone and heaved a sigh. It was past time to talk with Suzy. And now that she was safe and warm here in this wonderful cabin in the woods, perhaps she needed to take the first step.

* * *

Sloan spent a couple of hours checking out the supposed fisherman. He'd located a couple of rental cottages that were across the river from the cabin. Both of them were occupied. One had a minivan and kids' toys scattered around the driveway. The car at the other place carried Oklahoma license plates.

When Sloan scouted around the cottages, he spotted the man carrying a stringer full of bass up to the back door of the place with the Oklahoma car. Everything seemed right with that picture. But he copied down both license plate numbers and decided it wouldn't hurt to have the captain check them out.

He used a throwaway cell phone he'd purchased at a convenience store to call Captain Johnson. After he'd given him the numbers and some basic information on Lainie's welfare, he inquired after her sister's health. He knew Lainie would be eager to make sure her sister was indeed well, and home safe and sound.

"Suzy's physical health is good. You'd hardly know she'd been injured. But…" The captain hesitated and Sloan was immediately on alert.

"If she's concerned about Lainie, Captain, you may assure her that her sister is in good hands." After the words had slipped from his mouth, Sloan nearly bit his tongue thinking of how good Lainie had felt in his hands. But he didn't imagine that the captain would care to hear about how he'd misused his position as her protector. Sloan himself was still reeling from his breach of duty—and the fantastic results.

"I already have, Sergeant. That's not Suzy's greatest concern at the moment." The captain cleared his throat. "As of last night her husband, Jeff, was missing."

"Missing? As in deserted, you mean?"

"Too soon to know for sure, but apparently the two of them have had marital troubles for quite a while. None of the rest of the family has been aware of any of this, of course. And Suzy doesn't want Lainie to worry about her while she's going through all this upset and danger from the stalker."

"I understand, Captain. I won't reveal the trouble to Lainie. Suzy can rest easy about that." Sloan figured Lainie had plenty to think over as it was.

"Look," the captain began again. "The thing is, *I'm* the one that's most concerned about this disappearance. I always thought that Jeff Sampson married Suzy for her sister's money. It's occurred to me that the only reason he might take off now is that he knows something about Lainie's stalker that he doesn't want to reveal.

"For my money, his sudden disappearance is just too convenient."

Ten

At dusk, Sloan drove the SUV through the woods and parked in front of the cabin. The air was hot and thick with humidity. Thunder rumbled in the distance, and black, heavy clouds obscured the setting sun.

It had been a long, tiring day since he'd left Lainie, and the rash fury he'd felt when he'd last seen her was long gone. He'd given it a little thought along the way, and he'd come to the conclusion that embarrassment had probably been the biggest cause of his anger. But there was also the niggling sense that Lainie was too important to him—and that had been a large part of the reason why he'd felt so out of control.

He couldn't remember ever wanting anyone to understand him before, and had never cared what people thought. But this one woman changed everything.

Could there possibly be a future for them? Try as he might, he couldn't picture the two of them together forever. Just as he also couldn't imagine *not* having her in his life.

But he had nothing to offer her. Famous and wealthy, she had a loving family and lots of friends. Her life just didn't seem to have any room for a Texas Ranger. Sloan had no one—except possibly an incarcerated father he'd never even met.

He wondered if she might be the kind of person who believed people didn't grow up far from their roots. After all, his father was convicted of murder. Would she think, like father, like son?

No. Lainie was too smart for that.

And it wasn't so much their money differences that haunted him, either. He had several good-size bank accounts back in Houston, there because he hadn't needed most of his paychecks over the years. What did he need money for? No home, no family. There wasn't much for a hardworking Ranger with few friends to spend his money on.

Still, Lainie was one of the biggest home-and-family types he'd ever known—and he was as close to a vagabond as a Texas Ranger could be.

Sloan unloaded the groceries and the takeout he'd picked up, and headed for the front porch. A flash of distant lightning reminded him that the weather was certainly changeable at this time of year.

Lainie opened the door, and his heart jumped when she came off the porch to meet him. Lordy mercy, but just the sight of her could certainly stir his soul. And that was one more thing that had never happened with anyone else.

"I assume, since I didn't get a page, that there wasn't any trouble today without me," he said with a grin.

Lainie tugged one of the bags out of his arms. "No trouble." She answered him over her shoulder as she turned and headed back up the porch stairs.

"Well, then." He followed her into the kitchen. "I guess you didn't miss my ornery mouth too much, either. You probably had a very peaceful day without me around."

Lainie set the bag down on the counter. "Is that an apology, Ranger Abbott?"

Sloan put the rest of the bags down on the kitchen table and averted his gaze. "Maybe."

She felt a tug in the vicinity of her heart and ached to touch him. "To tell you the truth," Lainie began as she tenderly laid a hand on his arm, "things were too quiet around here today, Sloan. I...missed you."

He'd bought groceries. Ever since Lainie had been old enough to remember, she'd longed for someone to help her make a home. Someone who would think to bring home food when there was none. Someone who would help with the chores and take some of the pressure off her shoulders. Someone who would be there when the day was done and it was time to relax.

But that someone wasn't destined to be Sloan. She'd known from the beginning that he led a solitary, rambling life. He wasn't the kind who would stick around after his mission was over, no matter what her heart desired.

They had no future, but that didn't mean she couldn't make the most of their present. She helped him put the things away, and then she set the table.

"Hope you like fried chicken," he said.

If she didn't, she wouldn't have mentioned it tonight. "It's fine. Let's eat."

A crack of thunder broke through the cozy atmosphere. "Does that noise mean we're in for some rain?" she asked as she passed the sack of biscuits and slid the paper off her straw.

"Probably. But hopefully not so much that it floods."

"Flood? Would it?"

"The Guadalupe has been known to overflow its banks after big spring storms," he explained. "But there are five hydroelectric power dams near Sequin that should help stop the rising water. When I was looking around outside, I noticed a high-water mark about fifty feet down the bank from the house. It doesn't look like this cabin has ever been flooded."

"Thank goodness." She took a bite of chicken breast. "So what do people come here to do besides fish?"

"Swimming, rafting, kayaking." He shrugged a shoulder. "Most water sports, I suppose. Mainly, I suspect they come for peace and quiet, and to get away from the cities."

She stuck her fork in the coleslaw and remembered the reason she'd left the city. "Did you find that fisherman? And did you talk to Chet Johnson?"

He swallowed a sip of soda and scowled. "Yes and yes," he said flatly. His eyes blazed when she frowned back at him. "Okay, okay. The fisherman looks legit. He's probably a tourist down from

Oklahoma City. According to the clerk at the country store, he comes every spring.''

She tried mightily to keep the smug, I-told-you-so look out of her eyes. ''And Chet? Did you ask what the police have learned about the stalker?''

Sloan tilted his chin and studied her. ''Your family is fine, Lainie, just in case you're interested. Suzy is home from the hospital and seems none the worse for it. They're waiting for your safe return.''

''Oh, uh, that's good. Thank you.''

''And as for the police,'' he added, ''they're working on a couple of possible suspects.''

Another crash of thunder and the rain began to pound against the windows. Lainie jerked at the noise and stared up at the light fixture when the lights flickered off and on.

''Did Chet think it would be much longer?'' Regardless of the storm, she wanted to know how long she had left with Sloan.

''No way of telling. Are you anxious to return to work?''

Actually, she hadn't given a second thought to her job since they'd left Houston. ''Not really. I'm sure whoever's got the job of finding my old columns is doing just fine. But…''

She polished off the chicken breast and eyed a wing. ''I was wondering if there would be enough time for you to teach me to fish. And I'd love to putter in the garden here. It looks like it needs some weeding and fertilizing.''

''You like gardening?''

She nodded and grinned. ''I used to. There just hasn't been enough time lately. We have a gardener back home in Houston. Even if I had the time, he wouldn't let me near his precious plants.''

Sloan reached over and lightly ran a finger down her jawline. ''If it clears off tomorrow, we'll go fishing, Lainie. But it might be too muddy to get into the garden.''

The look in his eyes changed, darkened. He'd left his finger resting against her chin. Now he started gliding his thumb over her bottom lip. The salty taste of fried chicken and the erotic feel of his thumb aroused her.

The storm outside grew wilder as the storm within built in intensity. When the lights went out for good, Sloan carried her upstairs. They made desperate love that night as the storm howled against the windows, both of them knowing that their days were numbered, both of them praying for a reprieve from the inevitable return to daylight and their usual lives.

''Easy there, sweetheart,'' Sloan chuckled and ducked as Lainie swung her rod out the kitchen door and barely missed his head.

With the morning sun and the return of their electricity, he'd found a closet in the utility room that was loaded with fishing gear. Patiently teaching Lainie the various components of a rod and reel while they sat at the kitchen table, he'd had to fight back the urge to clear it off and take her right there.

He couldn't seem to get enough. But he knew she must be achy and sore from their nights of lovemaking, so he shelved his lust and relaxed into gone-fishing mode.

''This fishing business sounds complicated,'' she

told him. "Are you sure I'm going to be able to learn it in one day?"

"Well, if you were trying to learn the art of fly casting, probably not. But we'll just pitch out a little bait using these spinning reels and see if we can't fool some of the fish into jumping onto our lines." He helped her find the right grip for safely carrying a rod. "Anybody can catch a fish, Lainie. I taught myself at age six. All it takes is a pole, a line and something to use for a hook."

"You figured out how to catch fish all by yourself at age six?" She sounded stunned.

"Sure. There wasn't anyone around to teach me, and I wanted to learn. I'd found a magazine about fishing that someone left at the restaurant where Mother was working. I couldn't read most of the words, but I learned a lot by looking at the pictures."

He made sure he had the right tackle box and followed her down the grade toward the river. "My gear that first time was not what you'd call professional—a twig for a pole, thread for line and a safety pin for a hook. But it worked well enough to catch a few pan-size fish, and then I was really hooked."

They reached the bank of the swollen river. "Looks muddy," Lainie said with disappointment in her voice.

"The storm boiled up the mud from the bottom." When he saw that she was preparing to go back toward the house, he held up his hand. "The fish don't care if they can't see you, Lainie. They'll still be hungry. And all this rain has made it easier for us to find bait. I was a little worried that we'd have to take a trip to the convenience store to buy live bait.''

Her face brightened, and the clear enthusiasm he saw in her eyes made him catch his breath. She was so open and free. So sure of herself and what she wanted. Though she might not be some people's idea of a raving beauty, Sloan thought she was absolutely stunning.

He caught himself rubbing absently against the ache that had appeared in his chest. Needing to back away from the edge of an emotional abyss, he leaned their rods against a willow and looked around on the ground nearby for his favorite form of live bait.

''We'll have better luck up on the hard pack near the garden. Come on.'' He motioned for her to follow him.

''What are we looking for?''

''Night crawlers.''

''What exactly are night crawlers?''

He found what he'd been searching for and held it up for her inspection. ''Worms. Nice juicy meal for smallmouth bass.''

''Oh.'' Her voice was hesitant, and the look on her face was slightly dismayed as she stared down at the long, wiggling night crawler.

But to her credit, she rallied when he picked up a gardening spade and bucket and began turning over the soil.

''Just look at all of them.'' She smiled as every turn of the spade brought up more live worms. ''How many will we need? Do you want me to help?''

''Let's go with a couple of dozen to start. This is

enough,'' he said as he returned to their tackle on the bank.

Sloan showed her how to put the small hooks they'd be using through the nose of a worm. He expected her to recoil from the twisting live worms like most women would. But as he'd noticed before, Lainie was not like most women. She had a strong spirit and the tenacity of a mother lion.

Once he had the split-shot in place on their lines, and each of their worms was solidly hooked, he cast his line out with one flick of his wrist. ''See? That's the way you want to do it. Pitch the end of your line upstream and let it drift back down toward us.''

When she tried to imitate his cast, the line on her reel balled into a huge rat's nest. ''Oh dear,'' she lamented. ''I screwed it up. I guess I'm not meant to be a fisherman.''

Sloan put his rod down and unscrambled her line in short order. ''Nonsense. You just left your finger on the line too long.'' He rebaited her hook, put the rod back in her hand and moved in closely behind her. ''There's a little finesse to it. Here, I'll show you.''

Covering her hand with his own, he opened the bail and flicked her bait across the river. ''There. See how it works?''

She nodded as she closely watched the line drifting back downstream. ''How will I know if I catch a fish?''

''You should feel a tug on the line. When that happens, you give the line a jerk...like this.'' He used his position behind her to show her how to set the hook.

But as he did, she leaned her back against his

chest and he breathed in her fresh-from-the-shower strawberry scent. Whoa. Big mistake. He was instantly hard again.

Gulping down a moan of frustration, Sloan backed away from her and picked up his own rod. "That's good. It's an easy, fluid swing, not a throw. Now, crank in the line and try it again on your own." He was grateful she was too absorbed with learning how to cast to take notice of his discomfort.

As he put another worm on his line, he decided that he needed to find something to take his mind off her body. And to get her mind off trying too hard with her rod and reel. Maybe he could relay a little bit of what Captain Johnson had told him yesterday. That should take both of their minds off their immediate problems.

While casting his line upstream, he kept an eye on what she was doing with her reel. "Did I tell you that the captain mentioned how well Suzy was doing when I talked to him yesterday?"

"Yes," she said as she easily put another worm on her own hook. "I believe you did say something like that."

He gave her a quick nod of approval when she held out her newly baited hook for his inspection. "Apparently, her wounds were all superficial. They bleed copiously at first, but they also heal quickly."

"Uh-huh."

Well, that little discussion didn't seem to make her forget about what she was doing. "Suzy's home now. Captain Johnson says you can't even tell she was injured."

Lainie reeled in her line and realized the worm she'd just hooked had already disappeared. "I'm going through a lot of bait. Am I doing something wrong?''

''You're working too hard at it, for one thing.''

She frowned at him and retrieved another worm. ''I'm not sure I know how to do anything the easy way.''

Sloan laughed and reeled in his line. ''Relax. This isn't supposed to be a difficult job that someone has to master as soon as possible. Try to think good thoughts while you let your bait float back downstream.''

When he noticed his own line was minus a worm, he headed for the bucket. ''At this rate, we're going to run out of bait in a few minutes. Maybe the fish are stealing the worms off our hooks. But the current is running so hard after the rains that we can't feel them hit the line. After the next couple of casts, I'll go dig up some more worms.''

Lainie tried to do as he'd said, purposely lowering her shoulders. But relaxing while she was standing this close to Sloan was proving to be impossible.

Besides, when he'd mentioned Suzy's condition, her own guilt had put tension back into her spine. She already knew perfectly well how Suzy was doing. She'd had a nice chat with her sister yesterday by phone.

Lainie had learned from Suzy that Jeff had been gone a couple of days. But as she and her sister had been talking, he'd come home, surprising both of them. So all was well again back at her sister's. When this was over, she and Suzy would finish their talk.

But Lainie really didn't want to see the disappointment she knew would be on Sloan's face if he found out she'd used the cabin's phone to call. Nothing had happened because of it, of course. Lainie was almost positive that it wouldn't be possible to trace her whereabouts from one or two calls with her own family. But still…it might have been too casual and she didn't want to upset Sloan when their time together was growing shorter minute by minute.

Sloan let his line glide out of the reel and placed it thirty feet upstream with one easy flick of his wrist. "See? Easy does it." He watched her jerk the rod up and her line landed no more than ten feet away.

"Uh…did you know that Suzy and her husband have been having marital problems?" he asked, obviously trying to distract her attention from her line.

He was distracting her all right. "No…yes… I mean, I just recently learned about that." Flustered by his topic, she stammered and lost her concentration.

All of a sudden, Lainie felt a tiny tug on her line, and the tip of her rod bowed toward the water. "Hey! What's wrong?" She jerked around to ask Sloan what had happened and, as she did, the line in her hand pulled tight.

"You've got a bite," Sloan yelled. He dropped his rod and came to help her. "Start reeling it in."

Within a few minutes a pretty fish with golden highlights on its back and a soft gray on its belly was flopping around in the mud at the edge of the bank.

"Wow! I did it. I caught a fish."

He beamed at her. "Yes, you did. You landed a

smallmouth bass. Catch one more and we'll have a fish fry for dinner.''

"No problem," she said rather smugly.

Sloan gently took the bass off her hook. "I'll take this one up to the kitchen." He reached down and handed her the bait bucket. "Use the last night crawler for now and I'll dig up some more on my way back."

She did as he asked and proudly baited her own hook. "Take your time. I'll have another one landed before you return."

"Cocky, aren't you?" he said through a grin.

She grinned back. "You betcha I am. I caught the first fish of the day."

He shook his head with a smile. "Beginner's luck." Sloan started up the bank toward the house. "Be careful while I'm gone. It's pretty easy to lose your footing on this slippery bank if you're not paying attention."

It'll be a lot easier to concentrate once you're out of sight, she thought. "I'll be careful."

For a full five minutes after he'd disappeared into the trees near the house, Lainie's wide grin remained plastered across her face. What a wonderful day this was. And what a great guy Sloan had turned out to be. His fishing hobby was great fun. Maybe she'd become a fishing enthusiast herself.

She concentrated hard on flinging her line up the river. With every cast, her line came closer to landing at just the spot she'd meant to hit.

From behind her, she heard Sloan rustling through the bushes on his way back. "That didn't take too long," she said without turning around.

"Take too long for what?" The different but familiar male voice came from her left.

Gasping with surprise, she swung around to face the intruder. "Jeff! You scared the life out of me." She kept her rod loosely in one hand and put the other hand to her breast to calm her pounding heart.

"Sorry." Her brother-in-law took a hesitant step out of the bushes toward her. "I didn't realize you knew how to fish."

"I didn't. But I'm learning." Suddenly Lainie sensed that something was very wrong. "What are you doing here, Jeff? Has something new happened to Suzy? How did you find me?"

He shook off most of her questions. "I was listening in on the extension while you were talking to Suzy yesterday." Scowling, he took another step in her direction. "I figured that eventually you would have to call her. You've always been so self-absorbed and demanding of her time. It would never occur to you that she might be tired and not want to talk to you."

A cloud obscured the sun, and Lainie was hit by a chill wind. "Give me a straight answer, Jeff. What are you doing here?" Goose bumps rode up her arms, and she tightened her grip on the rod to help keep her balance on the slick mud.

Jeff reached into the pocket of his forest-green windbreaker and pulled out a shiny black gun. "I'm going to finish what I started—all by myself. Those bastard hitmen I hired were clumsy fools. This time, you're going to be shot—and killed—by your elusive stalker."

Panic turned her brain to mush. Jeff? Her own brother-in-law was the stalker?

Her legs were frozen to the spot. But her knees knocked together so forcefully that it half surprised her not to hear the bones creaking. "You want me to die? But…why?"

"Think about it," he sneered. "I'm sick to death of you having all the power. You don't have any right to tell me and my wife what to do. Just because you rule all the money doesn't mean you rule us."

"What?" Stunned beyond words, Lainie was speechless. Where was this hatred coming from? And how had she missed it for all these years?

"From now on I'll be in charge of the finances," he growled. "And just as soon as Suzy inherits that two-million-dollar insurance policy you took out, she'll be the next one to go." He grinned, but the effect was dark and evil.

Jeff lifted his gun and pointed it toward her face. "You know, I think maybe Suzy's death will have to be an accident," he said carelessly. "I'm not too crazy about having to pull the trigger in a face-to-face confrontation like this."

He cocked his head as if talking to himself, then shrugged. "Oh, what the hell. One face-to-face shooting won't be all that difficult for me to live with. Especially not with a cool two million to make me feel better. Prepare to die, Lainie."

Eleven

——

"**D**rop your gun, Sampson." Sloan stepped out from behind the shrubs, planted his feet and slowly raised his weapon in both hands. "Do it now!"

Jeff swung his gun around wildly when he heard Sloan's voice. Lainie swung, too, but her intent was clearly to hit Jeff with her fishing rod.

Sloan would've much preferred that she'd stayed frozen in place and let him deal with Jeff. But trust Lainie to want to take matters into her own hands.

Instantly the scene shifted. And in a blur of motion, Lainie lost her footing on the slippery bank, shrieking as she began to fall. Jeff heard the scream, swung back and fired in her direction. Before his bullet could hit its mark, Sloan fired one round.

Sloan's aim was sure, and Jeff Sampson's life was ended with one bullet through the temple.

In three strides Sloan made sure Jeff was gone

and kicked his gun off into the nearby brush. He reholstered his own weapon and was at Lainie's side without taking a breath.

"Lainie!" The air whooshed out of him and he was on bent knees in the muddy water.

"Lainie, answer me. Where are you hit?" She lay motionless on her side at the edge of the riverbank, and Sloan spotted a reddish-brown stain beginning to bloom through the water.

"Oh, dear God. No!" he cried, as he gently lifted her in his arms. "Please, sweetheart. Don't do this."

Blood was everywhere—in her eyes, mingling and matting in her golden red hair. Her eyelids were closed, and Sloan quickly felt her neck for a pulse. He found what he was seeking and at the same time watched as she drew a shallow breath.

He felt his heart start pumping once again. "Lainie Gardner, you keep breathing. You hear me? You can't give up now. I won't let you."

Cradling her to his chest, Sloan pulled out his cell phone and punched in 9-1-1. After he'd given the paramedics directions, he tried to find out where the blood was coming from, but there was so much of it. Her life seemed to be ebbing away.

"No," he choked. Holding her to his chest, he tried to blink back the stinging mist in his eyes.

It had been nearly twenty years since Sloan had been to church, and even then he'd only gone to please his mother. But as he held her and waited for the ambulance, Sergeant Sloan Abbott tried to make a deal with God. "Save her, Lord. Don't let her die, and I swear I'll…"

In a few minutes his prayers were answered when the ambulance arrived. The paramedics stabilized her and told him her wounds were not life-threatening, but head wounds tended to bleed a lot. Nodding absently, he remembered saying those exact words to her not more than a few hours ago.

He watched her still body being loaded into the ambulance and tried to talk them into letting him ride with her. But by that time the deputy sheriffs arrived, so he had to stay and give them a statement before they drove him to the hospital.

He muscled his way into the emergency room just in time to see Lainie, with tubes and wires strung over her entire body, being wheeled down the hall. He thought he'd lost his chance to talk to her, but she caught sight of him as her gurney started around a corner.

She screamed his name. "Sloan! Wait! I need you. Make them stop this thing."

Her attendants stopped when she started to shout, and he ran to her side. "Shush, sweetheart. I'm here. They can hear you all the way back to Houston," he teased.

She reached out to him, and he tenderly took her hand—which was no easy feat, what with all the tubes and needles they had stuck in her.

"Sloan, thank heaven you're all right. What happened to Jeff?"

He looked down into her eyes and felt a strange twist in the vicinity of his heart. Her face was pale and swollen, and there was a bandage over her beautiful red hair.

"I'm afraid Jeff's gone, Lainie. I had no choice."

"I'm grateful," she said with a gulp. "I don't understand why I hadn't guessed he was such a jerk. I need to talk to Suzy."

"She's on her way. Along with your mother and Chet." Sloan wanted to tell her what was in his heart. But the words were so huge that they stuck in his throat.

The attendants eyed him and murmured something about needing to get her wounds sutured.

He straightened up and patted her hand. "You go on now and let them fix you up."

"You'll be here when I get out?" she asked with a tremor in her voice. "You're not leaving for Chicago just yet, are you?"

"I'm going to Chicago, but not today. I'll be here." He wanted to tell her that he *needed* to stay. To see for himself that she was really going to be all right. That he needed *her*.

But there was too much unknown ahead. And he was positive that the two of them were not destined to spend their lives together. After all, he wasn't sure where his life was leading.

"You rest easy, sweetheart," he said instead. "Just concentrate on getting well and we'll all be here, waiting for you."

Sloan stared at the last inch of beer in the glass he'd been holding and quickly downed it. In the past three weeks since Lainie had been shot, his life had been on a roller coaster. And things didn't look as if they were going to calm down anytime too soon.

A cocktail waitress named Meg picked up his glass and asked if he wanted a refill. He nodded, then checked out the great mahogany bar that took up a good portion of the room.

A TV set, playing an out-of-town Cubs game, droned in the background. But because it was midafternoon, there weren't a lot of patrons in the bar to pay attention. Sloan glanced around at the one or two business-suited men, who had come in for early happy hour, and felt out of place. He'd been here for an hour, sitting in a booth near the back of the place, waiting.

Only once or twice in his life had he ever been out of the state of Texas. But Chicago was simply a big city like Dallas or Houston. It didn't seem all that different—except for the complete absence of Stetsons. But this upscale bar, with glossy wood floors and upholstered chairs didn't have a thing in common with any bar he'd ever visited. For a second he remembered about Lainie's desire to visit a honky-tonk and sincerely wished he could trade this sophisticated saloon in for one of those familiar joints.

The memory of Lainie brought his thoughts back to the last time he'd seen her. It was the day she was due to be released from the hospital. Her sister had finished packing her things and had gone to see about getting a wheelchair to roll her downstairs to the exit.

He'd listened while Lainie told him about how she'd designed a way to send in her columns from anyplace in the world. But how she wasn't sure that she could give advice to others anymore, when she'd failed so miserably with her sister. She was thinking of giving up her job.

Her smile glowed, in spite of the stitches. Her eyes sparkled when she gazed at him, and he figured she'd never looked more beautiful.

"I've asked Chet to help me make an offer on the cabin," she told him. "I'm thinking of turning it into a bed-and-breakfast. I hope it won't need much refurbishing.''

She couldn't seem to sit still. The excitement rolled off her in waves. "You probably know more about construction than I do. I'd like your input on what needs to be done."

"Lainie…"

"Oh, if you don't know much about building, I'll pick your brain about tourism and what kinds of fun things we need to offer at the cabin. I'm sure I can figure out how to advertise, but since I've never been to a bed-and-breakfast, I thought you…"

"Lainie, slow down…"

"But I'm all set and ready to get back to Houston." She tilted her head and squinted her eyes at him. "Driving straight there instead of winding around still means we'll be on the road together for a few hours, doesn't it? We'll have plenty of time to talk about all of this then."

"I'm not going."

The smile in her eyes died. "You're not going back to Houston?"

"Suzy volunteered to drive you home. I've got a reservation later for a flight out of San Antonio to Chicago. I'll have to hit the road soon to make it."

"Oh? Well…" She turned her back to him and fussed with her suitcase. "You're off to find out about your father. That's good."

He wasn't sure what he expected from her, but her calm demeanor annoyed the hell out of him. He'd been hoping maybe she'd cry a little, or ask him to reconsider and stay with her a while longer.

No, he knew that wasn't the right thing for either of them. Leaving her was hard enough now. Later it would probably be impossible. And apparently she had figured out the same thing.

"In that case, I guess I should tell you how much I appreciate what you did for me." She turned and took his hand in hers. "You saved my life…twice. And you taught me how to have fun—how to take the time to see the beauty in roadside flowers and in slimy night crawlers. It's been quite an education. Thank you, Sloan."

"I'm sorry I can't stay longer, Lainie. But I need to finish what I started—for my mother."

She squeezed his hand. "Of course you do. And I'm really impressed that you're doing the right thing. I knew you'd have to get back to your own life as soon as you could. I'm just grateful that you stayed with me for this long. You changed my whole life."

"Lainie…"

But before he could grab her up and kiss her senseless, Suzy came back into the room with a nurse and a wheelchair. He helped settle Lainie into the chair and watched while she was rolled into the hall, keeping her chin high and her face blank.

At the elevator she turned to him. "Thank you for *everything*, Sloan. I'll never forget you." Then the doors closed and she was gone.

"Sloan?" The older male voice dragged him back to the present, to the Chicago bar, with its black-leathered booth and his half-finished beer.

When he glanced up, a man stood beside the booth. A man who had his same eyes and mouth. But thinning gray hair and permanent creases across a high forehead and around the eyes made it clear Sloan wasn't looking into a mirror. However, the resemblance was close enough to recognize his own genes.

"Robert Jensen?" He swallowed against a suddenly dry throat and stood up.

"Yes, Sloan. It's pretty plain that we're related, isn't it?" The man reached out to shake his hand. "Whether you're happy about it or not, I'm your father."

Sloan took his hand. His father's warm fingers wrapped around his, and he took another step closer.

"I...I don't know what to say," Sloan stuttered.

His father didn't smile or say a word, just stood there, holding Sloan's hand in both of his and scrutinizing his son's face. Sloan noted that Robert Jensen was an inch or two shorter than he was, but their lanky builds seemed the same. He also marveled at how his father was dressed, in an expensive designer suit and tie.

"And I don't know what to call you," Sloan mumbled.

His father's huge grin brightened his whole face. "Rob is fine until you get to know me." He let go of Sloan's hand and dragged him into an embrace. "But...someday...it would make me happy if you could call me Dad."

Sloan backed up. "Let's sit down and talk."

"Okay, son. I have a lot to tell you."

Sloan knew the basics already. He knew that Robert Jensen and Mary Jo Pluckett had married thirty-one years ago. One year later they had a son in Chicago and named him Sloan. Two years after that, Robert was arrested and tried for the rape and murder of Mary Jo's co-worker and best friend. Robert had been sentenced to forty-years-to-life, with no possibility of early parole for the crime.

And then, nearly twenty-two years later, DNA evidence had exonerated him completely.

''I can't tell you how glad I was to get your phone call this morning. I've been searching for you and your mother for eight years now. Ever since…''

''You were released from prison?''

''Yes. My parents—your grandparents—both passed away before I got out. They couldn't tell me anything about why Mary Jo left or where she'd gone. I imagined that she'd gone back to where she'd been raised in Texas. But that's a huge state to search.''

Rob's eyes became wistful and watery. ''It's hard for me to accept the fact that Mary Jo ran out because my parents threatened to take you away from her. I knew they didn't like her, but I never thought they'd go so far as to hire a lawyer for a custody battle after I went to prison.'' He shook his head sadly. ''I guess I'm glad I didn't know while they were alive. It would've been too hard to face them on visitors' days.

''And now you tell me my darling Mary Jo is gone forever. That I can never make it up to her. It may take some time before that really sinks in.'' He focused on Sloan again and his face brightened. ''But you…just look at you. The last time I saw you, I was changing your diapers and trying to teach you to throw a ball. And now…you're tall and strong… and a Texas Ranger, no less. I'm proud of you, son.''

Sloan tipped his chin in response to the compliment. He still wasn't sure how he felt about suddenly having a past...and a family.

"You're the president of your own company?" Sloan asked, trying to take the spotlight off himself.

"Yes. My grandfather started the company over sixty years ago. When I got out of prison, I found that my father had left me several large trust funds. So I really don't have to work for a living, I suppose. But I need to. I need to contribute." He smiled at Sloan. "You know about that. You're a lawman. You contribute more than I ever could."

"You don't resent the law enforcement community for locking you up unjustly?"

Rob shook his head. "No. I was just in the wrong place at the wrong time. No one was out to get me personally. Everyone just did their jobs the way they saw them at the time.

"That's what we all have to do. We all have to do what's right for us at the moment." He sighed, then took Sloan's hand again across the table. "Please. Please tell me about you and your mother. Where did you live for all those years, and how did you get along?"

Sloan slowly pulled his hand away. "I'll tell you all about us later. But first, tell me more about you and my mother. Where did you meet? Why did you get married? What about my grandparents' relationship with her?" The questions just poured out of him.

Rob relaxed back in his chair. "First things first." The look in his eyes turned wistful again. "Mary Jo was the prettiest girl I ever met. She had chestnut hair with eyes to match. And the longest legs and the sweetest swing in her hips when she walked."

Sloan blinked his eyes. This man was talking about his mother?

"Yes, well," Rob continued. "I was a senior at SMU at the time. My great-grandfather graduated from there, and our family still makes large grants to their Cox School of Business. Mary Jo was killing herself with a small scholarship and a job in the school cafeteria." He stopped and grinned at his memories. "Tough little cookie. She was making top grades as a freshman."

Sloan knew his mother was tough, no question. But he hadn't known she'd gone to college. "But why did you two get married? Did you, uh, was I an accident?"

"No, son. We wanted you very much. You didn't come along until we'd been married for a little over a year." Rob sat up and leaned forward over the table. "We got married because I didn't want to live without her. When we first met, we fought like crazy. Both of us so strong-willed and demanding. But then I finally figured out that we were too much alike and that's what made the mixture so potent. It was as if she was my other half. The piece in the jigsaw puzzle that just fit.

"I knew I'd never find anyone else that matched me so perfectly." Rob smiled again, only this time he directed that warmth toward Sloan. "Fortunately, your mother finally saw it the same way I did. And together we made an imperfect family—but we created a perfect son. I couldn't have asked for any better wife and son, Sloan. Or any better memories."

"You still feel that way about her after all these years?"

Rob nodded slowly. "Always." He studied Sloan across the table. "There's someone you feel that same way about, isn't there? You have that lovesick look in your eyes, too."

Sloan dragged his hands through his hair. "It doesn't matter how I feel. It wouldn't work."

"I said that same thing once," Rob said, then chuckled. "My parents were snobs. They couldn't stand the thought that their only son would marry *beneath* his class. I was sure that Mary Jo wouldn't want to marry into such a stuck-up family." He shrugged a shoulder. "But wonder of wonders, she loved me…the foolish woman. She wasn't about to let anyone tell us we couldn't be together."

Sloan's throat was dry, and he tried to clear it.

"Does this girl love you like that?" Rob asked softly.

Sloan found his voice. "I don't know…yet."

Lainie pushed back from her desk, where she'd been studying plans for remodeling the cabin and turning it into a bed-and-breakfast. Tomorrow the place would be all hers, she thought, with a mixture of elation and sadness.

"I'm nearly ready to go." Suzy rounded the corner and entered her home office with a swing in her step.

"Oh, Suzy. I'm going to miss you so much." Lainie stood and hugged her sister.

The two of them had spent the last month telling each other the truth. Now Lainie knew that her sister's marriage had been a sham from the start. It hurt knowing that Suzy had never felt close enough to confide her troubles. What kind of advice columnist couldn't even see her own sister's anguish?

Lainie wasn't sure what either of their futures might bring. But she was positive that their painful pasts were behind them forever.

Unfortunately, it did seem that the two of them shared a lot in common. Both of them had loved men who couldn't—or wouldn't—commit to them. Suzy's first great love had dissolved when the family had moved to Houston. He hadn't been ready to commit and had let her go. She'd married Jeff on the rebound and had regretted it immediately.

Lainie still couldn't quite believe she hadn't known what her sister was going through. She chastised herself for being a spoiled brat and knew she deserved whatever pain she had coming. And judging by what Suzy had said about still being in love with the man she'd lost, years from now the wound of losing Sloan would still be as fresh and sore as it was at this minute.

"I'll only be an hour or two away," Suzy whispered. "And the telephones are working between Sequin and San Antonio the last I heard." She pulled back and smiled. "We'll still talk. Maybe more than we ever did in the past. And Mom and Dad will be fine here with their friends."

"Yes, but—"

"I need this, Lainie. I have to learn how to be someone outside of your shadow."

Lainie felt a pang in her chest as she stepped to her desk. Going off to be alone to start a new adventure was something that her sister relished. Lainie should be just as thrilled about her life's changes. A new start was just what she needed.

If she couldn't have Sloan, then she should make a life on her own. It was long past time for her to learn to make life worthwhile by herself.

The front doorbell rang. "I'll go down and see who it is," Suzy said as she swung out the door.

"Tell whoever it is to go away," Lainie called after her. "I'm not in the mood to talk to anyone right now. I need to pack."

She plopped down in her chair and started riffling through drawers. The moving van would be coming in the morning to take her desk and a few other things to the cabin. She'd bought the place furnished so she'd be leaving most of her furniture here in Houston.

She was grateful that the previous owner hadn't wanted to take anything. Most of the things just seemed to belong in the cabin, especially the bed. Or maybe that was simply her memories making a fool of her again.

The soft knock on her office door gave her a start. Who would be bothering her that didn't know how busy she was this afternoon?

Lainie threw open the door, prepared to give whoever it was a lecture on timing. But the words went right out of her head, as did most of the air from her lungs, when she saw that it was Sloan standing there, Stetson in hand.

"Lainie—"

"What are you doing here?" she asked with a little more irritation in her voice than she'd meant.

The darned man would have to show up just as she'd been on the verge of tears over moving so far away from her sister. "Is there something else I forgot to sign? Another statement that the police need for some reason?''

She turned away, and Sloan felt a tremor of anxiety run through his veins. He'd hoped…well, he'd hoped she'd be at least a little glad to see him after all this time.

''No, Lainie. No more papers. I just wanted to talk to you.''

''I haven't heard from you in over three weeks,'' she muttered over her shoulder. ''You didn't even bother to call to let me know that you'd found your father. I had to hear it from Chet.'' She spun back to him and narrowed her eyes. ''And you didn't care to know that I made an offer on the cabin.''

She poked her finger at his chest. ''It closes tomorrow, for your information.''

''I know,'' he said quietly.

Oops. Wrong thing to say. She bristled, and he could swear that those brilliant green eyes were shooting sparks at him. Mercy, but she was beautiful when she was mad.

''How do you know? Have you been checking up on me?''

''Yes,'' he said simply and dragged her closer. ''I missed you.''

Her eyes widened and her mouth fell open. He cupped her chin in his hand. ''I came today because I know that tomorrow you'll be moving. And I was wondering if you needed some help with the cabin remodeling job?''

When she simply kept standing there and glaring at him, he started to panic. ''We make a pretty good team and I was hoping you'd, uh, consider making it permanent.''

"Permanent? You want to work for me?"

He smiled, then brushed his lips across hers. "*For* you. *With* you. *Beside* you. I need you, Lainie." He faltered for a second when she only continued to stare up at him. "I love seeing your eyes light up when I show you something new. I need you so we can learn how to laugh together. And I guess I'm addicted to having you make me mad, stirring my blood. I need you beside me in bed, at work...hell, everywhere."

Thank God he was holding her. He wasn't sure he could stand on these shaking legs alone. "You're the very best part of me. I love you, Lainie. I'm trying to ask you to marry me. To share my life. To make a family with me."

"You want to marry me?" she squeaked. "You love me?"

"I love you," he repeated. "I've been in love with you from the first moment I saw you standing in your office lobby that day the world exploded around you."

She remained speechless, and his throat tightened. "I'm not as good with words as you are," he said past a choke. "But if you'll give me a chance, I swear I'll keep trying. For the rest of our lives I'll tell you every day. I love you, Lainie."

"I..." She started to back out of his arms as tears streamed down her cheeks, and he panicked.

"Lainie, please. I never should've left you to go to Chicago. I wished a thousand times that you'd been there with me. I promise you I'll never leave you again." He took a deep breath. "Only, tell me you'll marry me. Say that you love me, too."

Finally her eyes lit up and she threw her arms

around his neck. "I do love you," she said and laughed. "More than anything. And yes, I'll marry you."

"Thank God." He kissed her then. A long, slow, forever kind of kiss. A kiss filled with his soul.

"It seems I've been waiting for you my whole life, Sloan," she murmured against his lips. "You are my other half."

He dragged her closer yet, closed his eyes and kissed her hair. *She loved him.* As ornery as he was, she still loved him.

Relief raced through him, fueled by love. He bent to whisper in her ear. "Even though we're too much alike in all the wrong ways and you'll probably be sorry more times than you can count, I guess you're stuck with me until the end of our days. I love you, you *danged, crazy-fool redhead.*"

*   *   *   *   *

#1579 THE BOSS MAN'S FORTUNE—Kathryn Jensen
Dynasties: The Danforths
Errant heiress Katie Fortune had left home and her oppressive lifestyle behind and began anew—as secretary to Ian Danforth. The renowned playboy was a genius in the boardroom. But it was his bedroom manner that Katie couldn't stop fantasizing about....

#1580 THE LAST GOOD MAN IN TEXAS—Peggy Moreland
The Tanners of Texas
She'd come to Tanner's Crossing looking for her family. What Macy Keller found was Rory Tanner, unapologetic ladies' man. Rory agreed to help with Macy's search—to keep an eye on her. But as the sexual tension began to hum between them, it became difficult to keep his *hands* off her!

#1581 SHUT UP AND KISS ME—Sara Orwig
Stallion Pass: Texas Knights
Sexy lawyer Savannah Clay was unlike any woman he'd ever known. Mike Remington hadn't believed she'd take him up on his marriage proposal—if only for the sake of the baby he'd inherited. Falling into bed with the feisty blonde was inevitable; it was falling in love that Mike was worried about....

#1582 REDWOLF'S WOMAN—Laura Wright
When Ava Thompson had left Paradise, Texas, four years ago, she'd carried with her a little secret. But her daughter was not so little anymore. Unsuspecting dad Jared Redwolf was blindsided by the truth—and shaken by the power Ava had over him still. Could the passion they shared see them through?

#1583 STORM OF SEDUCTION—Cindy Gerard
Tonya Griffin was a photographer of the highest repute...and Web Tyler wanted her work to grace the pages of his new magazine. But Web also had other plans for the earthy beauty...and they didn't involve work, but the most sensual pleasures.

#1584 AT ANY PRICE—Margaret Allison
Kate Devonworth had a little problem. Her small-town paper needed a big-time loan, and her childhood crush turned wealthy investor Jack Reilly was just the man to help. Kate resolved to keep things between them strictly business...until she saw the look in his eyes. A look that matched the desire inside her....

SDCNM0404